FORBIDDEN VIKING

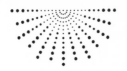

REE THORNTON

ACKNOWLEDGEMENTS

This book would not have happened without Rachel and all the WNW girls who critiqued multiple drafts and supported me throughout the editing process. I feel truly blessed to have such wonderful friends cheering me on. A special shout-out to Dana Mitchell, who played head-cheerleader on this project and dragged me kicking and screaming over the finish line.

DEDICATION

Till min mamma som är min bästa vän och som alltid har uppmuntrat mig till att följa mina drömmar.

A NOTE ON HISTORICAL ACCURACY

Forbidden Viking is inspired by historical fact with a heavy sprinkling of imagination.

Gottland (Gotland) is an island in the Baltic Sea with a rich history of Viking settlement and trade. Over the years, seven hundred hoards of Viking silver have been found on the island, however it was the largest, known as The Spilling Hoard, that inspired this story.

The Spilling Hoard was discovered in 1999 when a farmer uncovered a horde of silver coins and jewelry in a copper barrel in his field. The vast majority of the coins discovered were Arabic dirhams not brought to the island as plunder, but rather through far-reaching trade that connected Gotland with the Silk Road and its riches of silk, furs, and spices. As soon as I learned of the treasure that linked the known Viking trading center to the Far East, my imagination ran wild with possibilities of a story about an Arabian Princess and her Viking Jarl.

The World Heritage Listed medieval defensive wall that still surrounds Visby to this day is a remarkable sight. If only those stones could talk! The wall features in a few scenes in this story, however it was likely not completed until the 14th century, which is well after the Abbasid historical period, which inspired my heroine.

The Abbasid Caliphate (750CE-1258) was ruled by successive Abbasid Caliphs from the center of their power at court in Bagdad. In what is now known as the Golden Age of Islam (8th-14th centuries), Bagdad became a center of science, medicine, culture, education, philosophy, and technological invention. The scale and depth of innovation and advancement of knowledge during this fascinating historical period is astounding. Women faced many challenges under the Abbasid Caliphate; however, some women of wealth or noble birth were educated, took up professions such as medicine, and even published works of poetry. These women, many of whom became powerful figures, provided the inspiration for the feisty, educated Princess Samara.

CHAPTER ONE

VALEN

*V*alen Eriksson stood on the weather-beaten dock in the warm springtime sun and rolled his neck to ease the tension from his muscles. By the gods, he was weary, and the sun had barely passed the midday place overhead. It was both a blessing and a curse that Gottland's main port, Visby, was busier than usual these weeks before midsummer.

The piping notes of a golden eagle call rang out overhead as the predator swooped in a graceful arc and headed inland away from the gathering storm over the sea.

Freyr and her infernal timing! Now he would have to work in the rain to clear the longships moored at the docks either side of him and those that waited in the crowded bay for their turn to unload. He sighed. It would be another long day before he sought his bed.

The wooden dock creaked and rattled as he walked to the end. Another thing to add to his long list of repairs for when he was officially Jarl. He pulled the leather strap from his wrist and tied back the hair that was whipping around his face as the Kvitfjell longship glided to a stop beside him.

"Well met, Valen. It is good to see you," Dànel said, as his men threw off ropes and secured the ship to the mooring.

"And you. You are earlier than expected," Valen said, smiling fondly at the friend that had been absent from his shores far too long.

Dànel leapt onto the dock and walked toward him. "Njord was kind and filled our sail."

"That is good fortune," Valen pulled Dànel into a backslapping hug. "Did you get smaller, brother?"

His friend grinned and shoved him in the shoulder. "I have outgrown even you since I left the island three summers ago."

Valen scoffed and looked him up and down doubtfully. It appeared Dànel had a new attitude to match his enlarged body.

"You have the broad shoulders of a warrior, and that dark thick beard has replaced the fuzz of an adolescent boy, but I can still put you in a headlock to remind you who is bigger, *little* brother." No way had Dànel outgrown him, but his foster brother had almost doubled in size.

Dànel chuckled, looking every bit like his father Čuivi, who had been an elder of a Sámi clan that lived in the cold lands far to the north until he'd died three years ago.

"How is your brother?" He had heard reports that Dànel and Ándde fought often since Dànel had started captaining a ship in his brother's fleet after more than a decade living with the Eriksson clan. Sibling rivalry was to be expected after a long absence, but he had hoped Dànel would receive a fond welcome back into the family that had shunned him long ago.

Dànel shrugged. "Still stubborn and ill-tempered. I keep telling him that only a fool would enjoy living in a place so cold that it hurts to breathe."

"You whine like a hungry pup. You were fortunate to spend idle summers on our warm isle."

Dànel's fist flew out and hit him in the shoulder. "Idle! You worked me like a thrall."

He chuckled. The boy was still easy to rile. These last few years, he had missed the playful banter they'd shared as he had trained Dànel to live and fight as a Viking.

"And you learned well. Ándde spoke of your success in the north last summer."

Dànel huffed and crossed his arms over his chest at the mention of his older brother. "He enjoys sending me to lands where my eyelids freeze shut. I am glad to be back in warmer waters."

"As we are glad to have you, brother."

A deep clap of thunder rumbled in the distance as the wind moved from a brisk breeze to strong gusts that foretold of the approaching squall.

Valen glanced up at the dark clouds expanding overhead, an uneasy feeling settling in his gut. There was something unnatural in the way the clouds stretched across the otherwise clear skies.

"Come," he said, turning toward the shore. "A storm is brewing and I have much to do before Midsummer Eve. If I am lucky, the rain will pass quickly and I can work late."

Dànel wrapped his hand around his forearm, stopping him. "Valen, there was trouble in your waters."

He stilled, noting the concern on Dànel's face. "What trouble?"

Dànel stepped back and looked at him warily. "I know there is rarely strife in your territory—"

"Nobody has dared risk the wrath of the Eriksson clan in many years. Who would do so now?"

Dànel waved at the largest of his men still waiting on the longship deck. "Bring her."

Her? The hair on his neck stood on end as another low rumble echoed over the sea—it was an otherworldly storm approaching, a sign that the gods were at play with the lives of men. Why must they always meddle at the worst of times?

"A ship was raided."

He clenched his teeth. Raiding in his territory was an act of war. Was this a strike to test his position as Jarl before he'd even claimed it?

He saw none of Dànel's usual easy-going demeanor as he spoke. Instead, his body was tense and matched by the terse features of an equally grave mood.

"They took prisoners and escaped, but we pulled a survivor from the water." Dànel turned and nodded at his men. "Let her off. The rest of you can wait ashore. We shall unload the cargo later."

Dànel's men hastened to follow his orders and disappeared into the throng of traders hauling their wares to the market nestled safely behind the towering stone wall that protected Visby.

A small figure stepped onto the dock behind Dànel, her head lowered so the mass of dark tangled hair that fell in waves to her waist hid her face.

He peered around Dànel to get a better look, until his friend stepped aside.

Her hands trembled beneath the gray woollen blanket that she clutched around her shoulders and her small frame.

Óðinn! She was so small and slender it looked like she would be blown over by the wind.

"She is a mere child." He stared at her, his hands balling into fists. She'd likely been taken as a thrall or to be sold off at a slavers market. He couldn't stomach the trade of flesh, and had convinced his father to end the custom in their port after a slaver had killed Kalda. His clan had neither need for the dirty gold nor time for the unsavory characters of the sickening trade. On occasion, his father would free a thrall from aboard a ship and offer them a home on the island.

"I will wring the neck of the filthy cur that snatched a child in my waters."

Dànel shook his head. "Nei. She is no child."

Valen forced his body to relax and his jaw to unclench. Everything about this situation was off. He needed to uncover the truth so he could set this to rights. He could not have raiding parties in his waters, especially not with so many important guests coming to oversee his ascension to Jarl.

"Who is she then?" He must know so he could make reparations to her family for what had happened within his boundaries. And he needed to find the culprit and put a stop to this raiding at once.

"Come." Dànel's brow furrowed as he beckoned her forward. He murmured soft comforting words as he gently attempted to pry her fingers from the heavy blanket.

The poor child was terrified.

The thick mass of curled hair parted and she looked up at him, one dark eyebrow raised defiantly above eyes that elongated and tilted up on the outward corners around a dark amber center. Time ceased for a few moments, as the fire in her eyes stole the air from his chest.

Finally, the blanket slipped from her fingers and fell to her feet.

He swallowed hard at the sight before him. The oversized man's shirt she wore failed to hide shapely thighs and legs that were a tantalizing shade of bronze. Though small in height, the curves she'd hidden beneath that blanket were those of a grown woman. His eyes skimmed upward to where the shirt fell open at her neck to reveal the tops of breasts the color of warm rich honey.

Her breath hitched, and then she straightened her shoulders and clasped her hands gently across her waist as he forced his gaze up to lips that reminded him of the plump flesh of a peach.

"This is no Viking woman," he growled.

"Nei," Dànel agreed. "She's not."

He stared at the woman. Her amber gaze warmed him like

the sunlight gem revered by the seiðkonur magic women. A delicate design of swirls and dots decorated her bare feet. They were unlike anything he'd seen before, an entirely different hue to the markings on his own body.

"Who is she?" He didn't even recognize the raspy tone of his own voice.

Dànel shrugged. "She's not spoken a word. She jumped overboard to escape capture."

A brief flash of fear in the woman's eyes brought back images of his childhood sweetheart's broken body lying in the field, the deathly pale of Kalda's skin and the mottled bruises around her neck where her captor had strangled the life from her body. He flinched, and then forced his expression back to one of unyielding stone. It still haunted his dreams. This woman could have suffered the same fate if she'd not escaped. Had she been a random capture? Or targeted like Kalda?

He searched her face for answers, aware that her wary eyes followed his perusal. He stared at the small silver dot that adorned one nostril of her angular nose. He'd never seen a woman like her. He had no doubt that she came from a distant land.

"She is yours to protect now."

Dànel's words were the only thing that could make him tear his eyes away from her. "What? Nei."

"You must," Dànel insisted, his tone firm.

He shook his head and glowered at his friend. No way was he having this woman thrust on him. He had more than enough problems and duties in the lead up to the ceremony. "You found her. She's your problem."

As he spoke, her eyes darted around, taking in the many ships tied off to docks and the noisy crowd of traders preparing to ply their wares. Then she studied him, her gaze slowly following his jawline and lingering on his mouth, and when her eyes returned to his they were lit with such molten desire that he almost groaned.

Dànel pointed at the turbulent waves that matched the dark skies above. "She was attacked in your waters, Valen. It's *your* duty."

He forced himself to keep his gaze away from the tempting beauty. Dànel was right. He couldn't appear weak, especially not with all eyes on him until the midsummer ceremony. He had no choice—he'd have to keep her alive until he could be rid of her.

Her small shoulders heaved as she coughed and cleared her throat.

He crossed his arms and scowled at her. "How can I find her people to send her back when she doesn't even speak? She's probably mad as an old goat and they'd not want her back lestways."

Her eyes instantly narrowed, burning with the unmistakable fury of a woman scorned. She stepped forward, her lips opening slightly.

"Baaa," she spat at him.

Did she just bleat? He stared down his nose at her as his temper sparked to life.

Her tone was low and husky as her mouth effortlessly shaped words in his language. "A wise man would simply ask the woman, fool."

CHAPTER TWO

SAMARA

*T*he Viking's blue eyes widened for a split second, and then changed to a shade that reminded Samara of the dark depths of the ocean she'd crossed to reach this island. There was nothing soft nor kind in the warrior that stood before her. Everything from his arms wrapped in dark inked designs, muscular thighs supporting his solid stance, and the hard lines of his tense square jaw, held the irresistible allure of power. He was a leader among men, of that she had no doubt.

His nostrils flared.

A light drizzle began to fall as a shiver crept up her spine. The only thing Vikings loved more than the thrill of the chase was the kill, and she'd just made herself prey. Her heart hammered in her chest as she awaited his retaliation.

"She speaks." Now that he addressed her directly, the low rumbling growl of his voice held her frozen in place even more than his calculating glare.

The smarter you are, the less you speak, her grandfather's voice whispered in her mind.

Samara moistened her dry lips and wished she'd heeded the forgotten advice. She'd struck like a wounded cobra and ceded her only advantage. She wiped away the trail of water that ran down her cheek, aware that not even the cooling touch of rain would douse this man's anger now. Because of her recklessness, his goodwill had vanished like grains of sand through her fingers.

"If the wind blows, ride it, child."

She lowered her eyes. She knew that her survival depended on making this Viking an ally, so she would concede this battle to win the war. She lifted her gaze to meet his, confident that she could win him over. She had a lifetime's experience in the lies and deceit of court politics and knew the subtle moves needed to succeed in thorny negotiations. She could do this.

His sand-colored hair danced in the wind as he caressed his short beard thoughtfully, the gathering storm behind him matching his suspicious gaze.

She had to make this Valen see that she was no threat and need not be locked away. For the first time in her life, she was free, free of her handmaidens, free of her duty, and free of her father's ever-watchful gaze, and she would not let him take that from her.

"Já. I speak your language." Her eyes skimmed over the Viking leader's disapproving mouth and up to the fierce eyes locked on her. Her stomach fluttered, but then she firmed her resolve.

"How?" He crossed his arms over his chest, his sleeves rising to reveal more of the intricate knotted designs that curled around his muscular arms.

She wiped the rain from her face to stop herself from ogling his shoulders, which were as wide and imposing as the towering cobblestone wall behind him.

"My father taught me," she replied. Though she knew it was dangerous to display any interest, her eyes fell to where the hard planes of his chest were visible through his damp shirt.

Her stomach fluttered at the sight of the hairless golden skin of the man who controlled the city behind the wall.

"What is your name?" he demanded, snapping her back to reality.

She looked him dead in the eyes, thankful she'd learnt the art of deception as she schooled her features into the unreadable mask she'd perfected in the palace.

"Why should I trust you?" she asked, though she already knew the answer. She couldn't. She couldn't tell him she was a princess, the daughter of Caliph Radi al-Abbasid. She couldn't trust him, nor any other man. First, her father had told her that he would soon betroth her to a stranger, and then, Karim, the head of her royal guard, had betrayed her to her Viking abductor for a few chests of gold.

The Viking crossed his arms over his chest and growled at her. "You will trust because you must, woman. I will see to it that the man that attacked you is punished."

Her stomach rolled at the thought of the man with the fetid breath who had attacked her. He'd targeted her because she was an Abbasid princess, and planned to wed her to force her father to forge an alliance. She looked down at the wet timber beneath her feet. Vikings were monsters, and this one in front of her was no different. If he knew who she was he'd use her to try and gain advantage with her father too. She'd rather die than reveal her secret and risk being wed to a Viking.

"Your name," he barked, and the skies unleashed in a sudden downpour as though he had commanded it.

She ignored the rain that soaked the thin shirt she wore until it clung to her body. She must be careful—this man had a quick temper and was clever. No doubt, he'd see through any lies. She'd speak truths as much as possible. Perhaps if she didn't cause trouble, he would let her send word to her father.

His calloused palm cupped her chin and tilted her head back. Her heart thundered in her chest at his touch. She glanced behind him at the crowd scattering to take cover from the storm.

"Look at me when you speak. What is your name?" His blue eyes demanded answers.

She blinked at him, dazed by the sensations caused by his touch. "Samara."

"I am Valen, Jarl of Gottland. Where is your home, Samara?" His voice gentled and his thumb softly caressed her cheek.

Her breath caught in her throat. She pulled away from him, unable to think with his hands on her. "I travel with the court of the Caliph Radi al-Abbasid."

He pressed his lips into a hard line, clearly doubting her words. "Tell me what happened on the ship."

She looked away from him and welcomed the rain lashing her face. *How much could she tell him without revealing her secret?*

"We were attacked at night and separated from the fleet." She shook her head to banish the memory of the wooden deck covered in the thick red blood of her people.

When she looked back, he was watching her intently.

"They forced all the women onto their ship." She clenched her fists until her nails dug into the tender flesh of her palms. *The sword is swift for the traitor*—she would see Karim pay for what he had done to her companions.

"But you escaped." Valen prodded her to continue.

She brushed away the wet hair caught between her lips. "I threw myself into the water." She shivered as she recalled sinking below the surface into the inky blackness.

"She was half drowned when we pulled her out."

Valen's gaze shifted to Dànel and then back to her as his mouth formed a hard line. "Did you see his face?"

A shiver crept up her spine, leaving her feeling nauseous. She swallowed the lump in her throat and nodded. She'd never forget those soulless eyes.

"It was Leif Gustafsson." Dànel spat the name out like poison. His lip curled. "He flew no flag, but I saw him."

The change that swept across Valen's face was immediate. His eyes narrowed to slits, his jaw locked, and his teeth clenched.

Samara froze. She knew the signs of a man on the edge.

A vein in his neck swelled—she could see it pulsing as rage coursed through him—and he clenched his fists at his sides until his knuckles turned white.

She stumbled backward. She had to get away before he erupted.

His furious gaze softened as he registered her fear and attempt to put a safe distance between them. Slowly, the tension ebbed from his body and he met her wary gaze. The last remnants of anger faded from his features, once again replaced by the emotionless mask.

"Bring her, Dànel." With his order given, the massive Viking spun on his heel and was gone.

Samara felt his frustration in every shuddering jolt of the dock beneath her feet. She bit down on her lip until the painful throb reminded her that she was lost, more lost than the moon in winter.

CHAPTER THREE

SAMARA

*L*ater that night, Samara hid in the shadow of an apple tree, its long blossom-covered branches stretching out toward the edges of the lush green lawn where the Viking clan feasted.

She peered around the trunk at the two rows of tables on either side of the lawn that overflowed with feasting Vikings, and then at the long one beyond them that seemed to be for Valen's family and honored guests. Lanterns hung from branches over the tables, casting flickering light across a vast array of meats, fish, greens, bread, and fruits that lined the center of the tables.

"Have they no manners?" she muttered under her breath as she watched the Vikings gnaw flesh from bones and gulp down entire pitchers of ale. This was far from the hushed, orderly meals of the Abassid court. Though to be fair, beneath the shiny facade of courtly mealtimes, not even the Caliph was safe from the sharp tongues that wielded gossip like daggers against adversaries. They might be unruly, but from what she could see there was no devious pretense in these feasting Vikings.

Her stomach rumbled at the delicious smells wafting through the garden. She was hungry, but not enough to brave a mass of drunken Vikings. She shook her head and ignored her hunger. She'd watch from here and study their ways, especially their Jarl. She must know her enemy if she was to gain the upper hand.

She studied Valen where he sat at the center of the largest table, eating and chatting with Dànel. It was clear that the ceremony Dànel had told her about was a mere formality—this man already ruled his kingdom.

She watched him scan the crowd, his watchful gaze and somber disposition silently receiving the respect and obedience of his people. Then, satisfied that all was well, he returned to talking with Dànel.

She exhaled a sigh of relief. He'd not seen her—nobody had. She curled her toes into the damp lawn underfoot. A smile tugged at the corners of her mouth. It felt like walking on soft clouds compared to the dry sands of the desert. Precious water was never wasted on lawns at the palace. She'd often looked across the parched land that disappeared into the horizon, wishing for rain to make the scorched earth spring to life.

She plucked a blossom from above and leaned against the trunk, grateful for the safety of the shadows. Then she pressed the blossom to her nose, let her eyes drift closed, and inhaled the scent. *Divine.* The sweet smell was intoxicating.

Her eyelids fluttered open a few moments later to meet the deep blue eyes of the Viking Jarl across the garden—she'd been caught. For a charged moment she held his gaze. How long had he been watching her? A flush of heat spread across her skin, warming her like the sun's rays on a cold winter morning.

He motioned to Inga, the young woman who'd shown her where to bathe earlier and provided the borrowed dress she now wore.

Her chest tightened as Inga walked toward her hiding place.

She looked back at the newly constructed stone building where she had been given a small room, not much larger than a closet. She'd been relieved when she'd realized that the building housed the unwed women and children. Could she disappear inside and avoid Inga?

She turned back to find Valen still watching her, his eyes glowing with unmistakable warning. She shook off the thought of escape. It would not work—the Viking Jarl would never allow her to shun him.

"Come," said Inga, and beckoned her forward.

She let her shoulders sag as though defeated. She would let Valen think that she bent to his will while she plotted her escape. She followed Inga through the crowded tables. Inside, her heart thundered in her chest, but she held her head high and ignored the men taunting her with crude offers to join them in their furs.

Inga led her to the empty chair beside Valen and motioned for her to sit.

She baulked, then looked at the woman and shook her head. Not there. Surely, he would not want her seated in a place of honor. Unless... She dug her nails into the palms of her hands. Did he know her secret?

She glanced at where he sat, lounging back in his chair, one arm slung over the back as he looked at her with one eyebrow raised. He looked like a cat licking its paws after a satisfying meal, entirely too smug for her liking. She recognized his actions for what they were, a challenge. She'd done this often enough herself with strangers at court. He was toying with her, forcing her to action so that he could judge her response and glean information. It was a clever tactic, one she'd not expected from the rugged Viking.

"Sit, Samara," he demanded, his loud command ringing out over the noisy gathering.

Curse the man. She couldn't refuse and embarrass him in

front of his people—there would be no coming back from a slight like that. She sank into the chair beside him, unsure what was worse, that his deft manipulation equalled her own court-trained skills, or her sudden inability to breathe at the brush of his arm against hers. He'd seated her here for a reason. What did he want, and to what purpose? If he knew her secret, he could trap her here forever.

"Eat," he said, as Inga placed food and wine in front of her.

She sipped from the cup, letting the spiced wine soothe her frayed nerves. Now that he'd made escape impossible, she'd have to defend herself. She would start as she meant to go on—it was time to engage the enemy. She turned to face him. "My thanks for the food and clothing."

His brow furrowed as he studied her for a few moments from beneath hooded eyes. A heated awareness arose and then pulsed between them, making her skin prickle. Then he nodded curtly and continued gnawing the meat off a bone as though she didn't exist. His rude dismissal left no doubt that he had no liking for the unwelcome stranger in his land.

She released a shuddering breath. Her secret was safe...for now. She pushed her food around her plate. Her appetite had disappeared with the dozens of hostile eyes that followed her every move. She was not safe here. The longer she stayed, the more likely it was that they would discover her secret. Valen's people trusted her even less than he did. She needed to find a way off this island, quickly.

"Well met. I am Rúna Isaksson." A woman slid into the empty chair beside her and placed her cup on the table.

Samara studied the woman as she pulled a long flaxen braid over her shoulder to rest against the bust of the simple navy dress that dropped to her ankles, and then began to fill the plate in front of her. *What did she want?* Nobody ever approached her at court, except to beg her favor for their cause.

"You must be Samara. Dànel told us of your rescue and that you speak our tongue." Her green eyes studied Samara curiously.

She gave a welcoming smile. "Já. I am Samara," she replied warmly. This Rúna knew nothing of her royal status, she was likely just curious about the stranger in their midst. Her heart leapt at the realization that keeping her identity secret meant that she'd be seen for who she was, rather than her title. She'd always wanted a friend, but it had never been possible in the palace where everyone backstabbed and jostled for the Caliph's favor.

"Well met, Samara." Rúna relaxed back in the chair and drained her cup. "Where are you from?"

"Madinat as-Salam. It is three days' journey beyond Constantinople." A shiver ran up her spine. She could feel Valen's eyes on her. He was listening to her every word.

Rúna motioned for Inga to refill her cup. "I know of Constantinople. How did you come here?"

"I am a scribe. I have accompanied the Caliph on many trading journeys."

Rúna's eyes lit up and she spoke excitedly. "So you speak our language *and* you know letters?"

Samara nodded. "This is not the way here?"

"Nei," Valen snapped. "It is not."

She swung around to face him, her pulse jumping at his gruff tone.

His mouth was pressed in a firm line, his handsome face as hard as granite. She knew not why knowing his language and letters angered him, but it explained why he'd been so shocked when she'd spoken in his tongue. Had she erred in revealing she was a scribe? She loathed this feeling of being adrift at sea in this place where she did not know the rules.

"Ignore him." Rúna patted her arm, reclaiming her attention.

"Best let men think they are wiser, though we women know the truth," she said, and then grinned and winked mischievously.

She smiled at the woman's playful jest. Rúna was just the sort of friend she needed, someone strong and unafraid of Viking men.

"You must meet Ásta." Rúna motioned at someone across the room.

Samara watched as the serving girl in a simple gray dress moved toward them with an ethereal grace. Even from a distance, she could sense a dark sorrow in the woman's slow deliberate movements, as though the pain of the past reminded her to tread carefully through life.

"Samara, this is Ásta," Rúna said when the woman stood beside her, still clutching a serving pitcher.

"Well met, Samara." Ásta's thin lips curved into a gentle smile as she looked down at Samara from beneath thick brows. She had several small braids scattered amongst the auburn hair that tumbled to her waist like a waterfall, and brown eyes that shone like the skin of a plump juicy date.

Samara smiled and nodded in greeting. Ásta was beautiful, but up close, it was even more apparent that the striking facade hid a wounded darkness beneath.

Ásta leaned over and refilled Rúna's half-empty cup.

Was she a Viking thrall? The woman's skin was pale and smooth with a smattering of freckles across her cheeks and nose. A slave would have rough hands and dark skin from hours of toil in the sun. Ásta must be a free woman. So why did she serve Rúna?

"Ásta, Samara is alone here. If I ask Mari to assist me, will you help Samara since you understand how frightening it can be to be amongst strangers?"

"Já. I will show her our ways."

Rúna clapped her hands together. "Wonderful! We must all

meet in the morning. I want to hear all about this land where women are learned, Samara."

Before she could reply, a hush fell over the crowded tables as four towering men dressed in full battle gear strode across the grass toward them.

"Who are they?"

"Eriksson sons," Ásta whispered.

"Valen's brothers, my brothers by marriage," Rúna replied. "I married Jorvan Eriksson, three years ago."

Samara couldn't pull her gaze from the approaching Vikings. Each man wore a thick fur coat, had a rawhide bag slung over a shoulder, and had various axes and swords secured with leather straps across their backs. The air around the warriors crackled with carnal promise. She'd never seen so many handsome men in one place. Were all the men on this island like this?

Her pulse jumped. Two of the men were identical twins with hair the color of a burnt orange sunset as it kissed the horizon, and matching red beards. Twin souls! It was a rare blessing for a family.

Valen rose beside her, and then walked around the table. "Ivvàr, Rorik," he said, nodding in greeting.

"Valen," the twins replied in unison.

When he turned his attention to the two other men, she studied them closer.

One had his fair hair tied back, leaving the dark ink design that covered his shaved skull over his left ear visible. The other had the hair shorn close to the skull on one side and a mass of light hair that fell in gentle waves below his ear on the other. His face was covered in a thick beard and the barest peek of an inked design was visible on the back of his neck.

Valen nodded at them. "Njal, Erik. My thanks for your haste."

"We leave with the tide," the bearded one said, his voice a deep rumble.

Valen nodded and looked back at the twins. "Ivvàr, Rorik.

Find Leif Gustafsson. He was last seen heading south. He will answer for raiding in Eriksson waters." His words cut through the silence of his clansmen, reassuring them that he would have vengeance for the slight to his people.

She fell back in her chair. He was sending someone to capture her attacker. Her pulse hammered as the crowd erupted. Their fists pounded tables and they drained their cups in solidarity with his order.

When the noise eased, Valen continued. "Erik, Njal. Find the Caliph's fleet, and tell him that he may collect his scribe if he wishes her return."

A wave of relief swept over her. Her father would come for her—she would soon be safe.

"May Njord fill your sails and protect you. Hasten back before Midsummer Eve." Valen pulled each of them into a back-slapping hug, and then stood watching until his brothers disappeared back into the night and the feasting resumed.

She studied the wide expanse of his shoulders and the flickering gold of his long hair. This man was nothing like the tales of cruel Vikings the travelling bards had brought to the Abbasid court. His response to her arrival had been as carefully considered and fair as any judgment by her father. He was not ruled by explosive violence and a thirst for blood, he was clever and careful, and that made him dangerous in a different way.

He turned on his heel and pinned her with a pensive look.

Her breath hitched. It felt like he could see inside her, that his eyes as dark as the sapphires that decorated the royal palace could mesmerize her into spilling her secrets. She broke free of his magnetic stare and slowly lowered her head. Regardless of his distaste for her, he'd done her a favor and she would acknowledge the aid he offered. Raising her head she met his gaze once more, her heart thundering in her chest as she waited for his response. Would he acknowledge her silent thanks, or rebuff her again in front of his people?

His mouth remained in a hard line.

Her heart sank. It seemed unlikely that she would win over the cold distrustful Viking.

His head jerked once in a curt nod before he turned away.

She sighed. It was a start.

CHAPTER FOUR

VALEN

*V*alen's gaze drifted toward Samara, drawn to her like a bee to honey. No matter how hard he tried to resist, the pull between them was undeniable. He couldn't have her, not when he must soon choose his Viking bride. He'd known she was trouble the moment he'd laid eyes on her.

He glanced sideways at where she sat beside him, her back straight and her head held high as she sipped at a cup of spiced mead as though perfectly at ease with her situation. He huffed and looked away. How was she not a cowering and trembling mess in a gathering of armed and dangerous Vikings?

"Is something wrong?" she asked, speaking quietly to not be overheard.

He glowered at her. "You blow in with the storm and now the whole clan is in a stir. Everywhere you go trouble follows."

She recoiled at his harsh tone, the red wine in her cup coming perilously close to splashing over the rim before she composed herself and placed it gently on the table.

"What does that mean? I've caused no trouble."

He scoffed at her bewilderment. "Your presence alone causes

trouble. Do you not hear the women whispering of evil and curses as you pass?"

"They do?" she stammered, and he couldn't miss the flash of fear in her eyes.

"Já. And just this afternoon I had to lay claim to you to stop my men from fighting in the training yard over who would bed you first."

He'd told himself he'd claimed her to protect her from his men, but now he couldn't deny that she'd intrigued him and he was curious to learn more about her. His chest tightened. He couldn't become attached to her, to *any* woman. When he became Jarl he would choose a bride that strategically benefited his clan, the daughter of another Jarl. He'd always known this was his fate, and he was prepared to do his duty.

He watched, fascinated, as the color drained from her face, yet somehow her expression and demeanor showed no signs of cracking. Indeed, he would have thought her entirely unmoved if not for her ashen pallor and the slightest tremble in her bottom lip. An unstoppable surge of admiration filled him. Despite all she had endured and the dangers of her current situation, she still refused to be broken.

"Now I will have to keep you with me for your own protection until the Caliph arrives for you." He hoped the renowned Caliph Radi al-Abbasid would arrive soon so he could hand her over and get back to focusing on what was important—securing Gottland's future.

"My days are busy so try to stay out from under my feet."

A flash of anger lit her eyes, and then she nodded briskly. "I will be no trouble. I am sure the Caliph will come for me soon. Gratitude."

He tilted his head and looked at her, making no effort to hide the fact he was trying to figure her out. Had her earlier thanks that he'd rudely brushed off been genuine? His meal formed a lump in his stomach. None of this was her fault and he'd treated her unfairly. He should offer her some comfort.

He leaned closer, inhaling the soft scent of soap on her skin and the lingering fragrance of flowers on her hair.

"You are safe. My brothers will capture Leif Gustafsson and he will be punished."

Her intent gaze caused a surge of heat in his blood. By the gods, it had been years since a woman had affected him like this.

"You know this man Leif?"

He watched her mouth as she formed the words in a husky whisper. Then she swallowed and his eyes fell to her neck, to the telltale pounding of her pulse hammering beneath the skin. Satisfaction filled him—she felt this tug of desire between them too. It was a struggle to force his eyes upward and his mind back to her question.

"Já. I know him." It was his duty to catch whoever was raiding in his waters, but in truth, he was doing it for her as well. Trouble or not, he wanted to protect her.

"How shall he be punished?" As she spoke, her slender fingers tightened around her cup of wine on the table.

"In the Viking way," he said, avoiding her question. No need to frighten her even more. "No one raids my waters twice."

She lifted the cup to her lips and sipped, her eyes never leaving his. "It seems the tales of violence are well-deserved," she said, and then turned away and lifted a spoonful of stew to her lips as if the thought didn't bother her in the least.

Who was this woman who thought she sat amongst savages yet showed no fear? He wanted to probe further, but she'd settled into a comfortable silence as she ate. He downed his ale and returned to his half-eaten meal. He'd not interrupt the quiet.

"Valen?"

His head snapped up as the port-master led a stranger toward his table. "Finne?"

"Sorry to interrupt your meal. This trader arrived late today, but none understand him. I thought you might?"

He laid his dagger on the table and motioned the stranger forward, noting that the man's garb was that of a simple fisherman with little adornment or clues to his origin.

"Well met." He raised his hand and greeted the man.

"Salevete." The man bowed his head in greeting. He continued speaking for a few moments, and then paused when he realized he was not being understood.

"Nei, Finne. I am unfamiliar with this tongue too." He motioned for his cup to be refilled and considered the options, though he knew there was but one. Trade without a shared language was an arduous process. He would have to handle these negotiations himself.

Beside him, Samara shifted in her seat. "May I?" She motioned at the trader with her long graceful fingers.

May she what?

After a few moments in which he did not respond, she raised her hand to greet the trader. "Salve, Xaris."

He watched her lips stumble over the guttural sounds. How many languages did this woman speak?

She continued talking for a while, nodding and smiling when the trader responded eagerly to her with an extended chatter of foreign words.

He listened attentively, trying to find familiar words or phrases within the unfamiliar rhythmic patterns of their speech, but his patience ended when Samara laughed and the trader glowed with obvious pride. Enough was enough—he refused to be excluded from conversations in his own hall.

"What does he say?" he demanded.

She turned to face him, reprimanding him with her eyes before she answered. "He is a Roman. His name is Xaris. He has come to trade."

His jaw clenched. The woman balanced precariously on the

edge of deference and insult with as much deftness as the nimble-footed boys that were sent up to secure a ship's rigging in a storm. "How do you know his tongue?"

She shrugged casually. "I had a tutor."

"A tutor?" He narrowed his eyes. Only the wealthiest families provided tutors, and only for their sons. Was it so different in the east?

"It is not uncommon. I studied languages, art, astronomy, medicine, and letters. Latin was one of many I learned for my role as scribe. The Caliph frequently trades with the Romans."

"You are learned in many areas?" he said, cursing himself when he heard the distinct upward inflection that betrayed his shock. Nothing about her made sense.

Her brow furrowed in response to his obvious surprise, and then she nodded. "As are many women of the Caliph's court."

He shook his head in disbelief. Most of the *men* he knew did not even know their letters. He sat back and studied her.

She crossed her arms and arched one eyebrow. There was nothing weak or foolish about her, she was strong, smart, and comfortable being in control. She was no obedient servant. Who was she?

He brushed the question aside for later contemplation. He'd felt the subtle shift in power when she'd realized she'd surprised him with the Roman. Eventually he would have to remind her who was Jarl, but for now he needed her help.

"Would you translate for the Roman in our negotiations?"

A flash of surprise crossed her face, and then her shoulders relaxed. "If you wish."

"I do." He motioned at the Roman that still stood waiting, watching their entire interaction. "Invite him to dine and tell him we will trade in the morning."

She turned to the Roman, smiled warmly, and spoke once more.

"Please get our friend food and drink," he instructed Finne, knowing the man would ensure the Roman was fed and housed beyond the wall with all the other traders.

He turned sideways in his chair to face Samara. "You enjoyed speaking with the Roman?"

She looked at him warily, pausing to weigh her answer. "It is nice to practice other languages—otherwise I will lose the skill. Do you not find it is so?"

"I could not say. I speak with many traders daily." He kept his expression blank, wanting to keep her off balance, needing to claw back some of the control that seemed to vanish every time she opened her mouth.

"I knew many languages as a child, but my elderly tutor died when I was eight and his replacement was not as learned. Without regular practice I lost much of what I had learnt."

He knew all too well the power that came with knowledge. He'd been taught alongside the sons of other Jarls. He couldn't have Samara think herself his equal and question his command because she was more learned. A Jarl must never lose the upper hand—he needed to correct the balance, fast.

"You surprise me," he said, giving her the penetrating stare he used to bring his wayward warriors to their knees.

Her lips twitched at the corners. "I do not imagine that would be very difficult, Viking." She raised her cup in a silent salute and drank.

He blinked hard. How had the troublesome woman bested him yet again?

CHAPTER FIVE

VALEN

Six days later, Valen downed his ale and crossed his legs beneath the table in the unusually empty longhouse. He was glad to have a full belly and a moment to rest in peace before he met Finne at the docks.

"Well met, Ásta."

Rúna's handmaiden stopped sweeping, holding the broom motionless in one hand as she spoke quietly.

"Jarl." She inclined her head in greeting. "Samara is not with you? Does she require a meal also?"

"Nei. She dines with Rúna and the other women in the garden." Earlier, he had requested that Rúna keep watch over Samara for a while, content in the knowledge that any man that even attempted to approach her would feel the bite of the fierce shield-maiden's sword.

Ásta nodded and continued sweeping the dust from the corner of the room.

His thoughts returned to Samara. True to her word, she had stayed out of his way and been no trouble these last days. Without speaking it aloud, they had both chosen to ignore the tug of desire that pulsed between them and had fallen into a comfortable companionship as he'd answered her endless questions about clan life and the settlement. His lips curved up at the corners as he thought odd the woman with an insatiable thirst for knowledge. Surprisingly, he'd enjoyed how her questions made him see Viking life through her eyes. The warm cadence of her voice was like a soft caress in his mind.

Why are the smallest children sent to haul heavy wooden buckets of water from the stream? To whom do the stray dogs that wander the village streets belong?

Blood rushed to loins at the memory of her petting the small mangy dog and looking up with those wide questioning eyes. His attraction to her had been building, but in that moment he'd wanted to push her up against the wall of the nearby cottage and kiss the kind-hearted woman senseless.

Loud shouts and a slew of foul cursing filtered through the open door along with the thundering footsteps of an approaching crowd.

What the Hel? He leapt to his feet and gripped the hilt of his sword, anticipating trouble.

Ivvàr and Rorik stormed through the door and crossed the room hauling a struggling man between them.

His hand fell from his sword and he relaxed at the sight of his brothers. They had the situation under control, though they did naught to quell the bloodthirsty jeering crowd that had followed them inside.

He walked around the table and studied the target of such fury. He recognized the man's massive build and dark hair— Leif Gustafsson. Satisfaction and brotherly pride filled him. He'd known the twins would return with the accused raider. None could outrun the most gifted longship captains in his fleet.

The captive cursed and kicked out violently as Ivvàr and Rorik shoved him to his knees in the middle of the room. That the man behaved so when surrounded by enemies and little

chance of escape told him everything he needed to know—the
man was unhinged.

He raised his arm to silence the angry crowd, then crossed
his arms over his chest and nodded at his kin. "Brothers. I see
you have caught the raider."

"We found him and the other captives." Rorik's mouth was
twisted in the angry snarl that rarely seemed to leave his face.

He searched for Rúna's handmaiden and found her pressing
herself against a wall with the broom clutched in her hand.

"Ásta, bring Samara here."

She nodded and hastened out the door.

Then he turned back to his brothers. "Where?" he asked
Ivvàr.

"South. Nearing his brother's lands in Gottar. The women
are being tended to by a healer. It will be a while before they can
travel here."

Valen shook his head at the traitor that was so unlike his
well-respected kin. For decades, the alliance his own father had
forged with the Gustafsson clan had been vital to keeping the
peace on the seas and the trade flowing to Gottland. Just yester-
day, Leif's brother, Jarl Siv Gustafsson, had arrived as an
honored guest to witness his own ascension to Jarl. He couldn't
afford to make Siv Gustafsson an enemy, but he couldn't ignore
the wrongdoing and insult to his clan either.

"First Rúna's wedding and now raiding in my waters. This is
the second time you have taken on an Eriksson and failed."

Leif glared up at him through the slits of his two swollen
black eyes.

Valen couldn't summon any pity for the man he knew had an
unnatural thirst for blood and a reputation for torturing the
weak and innocent. A beating from the twins was far less than
what he deserved.

"You are accused of raiding in my waters. You will face
judgement."

"VALEN!" Siv Gustafsson ran toward him, clad only in his breeches, his sword drawn. Even in the dim light of the room, the Jarl Gustafsson's much-feared blade appeared as long and sharp as it was in the songs of the travelling bards that told of its many battles.

In seconds, Rorik and Ivvàr has their swords pointed at the furious Jarl.

Siv skidded to a stop and glared at the twins. The legendary battle scar that crossed his bare chest from his neck down to his groin demanded respect. The man was a seasoned warrior with a devoted army.

"Release him," Siv roared, his usually friendly mouth twisted into an angry scowl.

Valen gritted his teeth and quelled his rising temper. This was exactly what he had not waned to happen. The air in the longhouse was thick with the tension of predictable violence. He needed to find a way around bloodshed...fast. He waved off Rorik and Ivvàr.

The twins stared back at him stubbornly. Backing down from a fight was not in their nature.

"Brothers," he snapped in a tone that brooked no argument. "I will not have bloodshed before I speak with Jarl Gustafsson."

Ivvàr shook his head and stepped back. He was the more level headed of the twins, but Rorik was the concern.

Rorik was struggling to control his unruly temper—he looked like he wanted to take Leif's head off. Thank the gods he'd sent Ivvàr with his twin, or he'd likely be looking down at a headless corpse right now. Rorik needed to learn to control his dark urges, and soon, because Ivvàr would not always be around to stop him.

"Rorik..." he said in warning.

Finally, Rorik flexed his fingers on the hilt of his sword, and then he spun on his heel and stormed out the door.

An arrogant smirk spread across Leif's face.

He believed he was untouchable because of his powerful brother. He thought Siv's arrival had turned the tables, but he was dead wrong.

Siv gripped Leif's forearm and pulled him to his feet. "How dare you insult my brother like this?" he said, as he cut the ropes that bound his brother's hands.

Valen crossed his arms and glared at the smug traitor rubbing his chaffed wrists. "Are you going to tell him, or shall I?"

CHAPTER SIX

SAMARA

*S*amara wiped her sweaty palms on her dress and
followed Ásta toward the longhouse. What did Valen
want? She'd only left him a short while ago to spend the afternoon in the garden with Rúna. He'd not mentioned it, but she
knew having her around made it harder to complete his many
duties.

"Quickly," Ásta said, rushing toward the open door. The
whole island seemed to be moving at a frantic pace these last
few days. The warriors hunted, hauled wood, and added even
more tables to those in the garden, while the women scrubbed
chambers clean, washed linens, and toiled night and day under
orders of the cook that never seemed to sleep.

Samara stumbled to a stop in the doorway. She'd never been
inside Valen's home. Why would he call her here?

"Come! He is waiting," Ásta hissed, waving for her to follow.

She took a deep breath and stepped through the longhouse
door, pausing on the threshold to allow her eyes to adjust to the
dim light cast by a smouldering fire in the hearth.

Her eyes darted around the crowded room, taking in the
elevated beds strewn with furs lining the walls, and the woven

tapestries that hung from beams on the left, creating a private chamber.

Every head in the crowded room turned when Ásta side-stepped, and she felt pinned in place by the Vikings lining the walls. Her skin prickled as she spotted Valen standing in the center of the room amongst a group of men. The burst of heat she'd become adept at hiding these last few days flared to life when his smouldering blue eyes met hers.

"Samara, come here." He motioned her over.

Hushed whispers of the onlookers fell to silence.

As she began to move the other men turned to face her.

A bare-chested stranger holding a sword at his side, one of the flame-haired twins and…

A strangled cry escaped from her throat. There stood the Viking that haunted her dreams, grinning at her. She stumbled back, her hand flying to her throat as the memory of his fingers squeezing her there came flooding back.

Ásta's hand pressed into her back and pushed. "Go to him," she hissed.

Go to whom?

"Samara?" Valen said, his brow furrowing with concern.

Everything inside her screamed to run, to put as much distance as possible between her and the monster, but there was no escape.

"Samara, come here," Valen said, urging her forward.

Her heart raced as she crossed the room on shaky legs. She skirted the wall, keeping as far away from her abductor as possible, bile rising in her throat as his venomous green eyes stalked her every move.

He had darkening bruises on his face, and chaffed wrists where he'd been bound, but there was no mistaking the evil glint in his eye. He'd been caught, but not conquered.

She stopped beside Valen, grateful for the safety she felt in his presence, yet unable to tear her eyes from the threat in front of her. Why wasn't he in chains? Didn't they know how dangerous he was?

"Your brother raided in Eriksson waters, Siv. We have a witness," Valen said. "Samara was on the ship that was attacked."

The bare-chested warrior turned to his brother. "Is this truth?"

Leif kept his eyes locked on her and remained silent.

"He was halfway to your lands with his haul of women and loot when we caught him. Another twenty witnesses will arrive here soon," Valen continued.

The air rushed from her lungs at his words. Her people hadn't been sold as slaves. Despite the horrors of what they had endured, they'd lived, and she vowed she would see them safe once more.

The shirtless stranger's jaw had hardened as he listened to the accusations against his kin, then he turned to her, his expression fierce and demanding.

"Is this true, woman?"

Her eyes flicked to his brother. A shiver crept up her spine. She knew that look—it was the warning before the cobra strike. If she spoke the truth, Leif would kill her. Her pulse hammered in her chest. What should she do?

"Samara." Valen's sharp tone broke through her thoughts.

She looked up at him in a daze.

He stood beside her, his feet shoulder-width apart and arms crossed loosely over his chest. His calm demeanor saying he was in complete control, and that she had nothing to fear. He nodded in encouragement.

She had to do this. If she didn't then he would escape punishment, and that crazed look in his eye told her that he would never stop hunting her. She sucked in a fortifying breath and squared her shoulders.

"They speak truth." She pointed at Leif with a trembling

finger. "*He* attacked our ship at night, killed all of the men, and stole the women."

Leif's nostrils flared and his lips pulled back, baring his teeth at her. She couldn't miss the whites of his bulging eyes nor the tension in his corded neck as his eyes threw daggers at her.

"You will pay for that when you are my wife."

"La." The denial fell from her lips in her native tongue. "Nei," she repeated so all could understand, her confidence buoyed now that she'd realized he could no longer hurt her. Speaking out against him had sealed his fate. Now he'd be locked away, and she'd never have to fear him again.

"I would rather die than be your wife. No man shall force me to wed."

"You. Are. Mine." A shower of spittle flew from his mouth as he yelled.

"ENOUGH!" Valen roared. "You raided in our waters. Attacked the Caliph's fleet and stole the women, this woman..." He pointed at her. "The Caliph's personal scribe."

Leif's green eyes narrowed to slits, and then flicked back and forth between her and Valen.

She froze as she realized her error.

An evil smirk lit Leif's face.

Nei. She clutched her rolling stomach. It was over. He knew she had hidden her identity from Valen. Her chest tightened until it was difficult to breathe. Leif knew that she was a prize the Viking Jarls would fight over, and if he couldn't wed her, he'd make sure someone did...

"Is that so, Princess?" Leif rocked back on his heels, as though delighted with the stunned silence in the room.

"What?" Valen turned to her. "Princess?"

She squeezed her eyes tight to avoid meeting his eyes. Valen had been kind this last week. She'd been sheltered, fed, and he'd personally seen to her protection. She'd thought he'd begun to soften to her, when last night at dinner he'd conversed openly with her in front of his clan. Now that he knew her secret...

Leif's elated cackle broke the heavy silence.

Her head snapped up, her instincts telling her to watch her enemy.

Leif thrust a finger at her, more spittle flying from his mouth as he threw the final verbal dagger. "She is *Princess* Samara, the only daughter of Caliph Radi al-Abbasid."

The watchful crowd inhaled an audible gasp.

Her heart sank as her deception was laid bare. If she were not so terrified of the vicious man, she would have used her dagger to render him as useless as a gelded bull.

CHAPTER SEVEN

VALEN

*V*alen stared at Samara in shock. Even in the dim flickering firelight, he saw her face redden as though burning with the flames of her hidden guilt.

"Princess?" He felt the backlash of his earlier ale. "Is this truth?"

Even as he asked it, he knew the answer. Everything puzzling about Samara suddenly fell into place and made perfect sense. The graceful way she carried herself, her reserved and tactful demeanor, her learning that far exceeded any man he knew. She was a princess.

"Samara?" He cupped her chin and forced her to look at him.

She pulled away and jutted her chin as she spoke without a hint of remorse. "It is truth..."

Óðinn! For the first time in years, he'd met a woman he actually wanted and she was a damned princess—a beautiful, infuriating, and untouchable princess. Loki, the trickster, was a cruel and devious god to toy with him so.

"I am Princess Samara Abbasid."

He took a step back as his temper flared. She'd lied. She was the daughter of the powerful Caliph that he'd long sought to trade with to secure his clan's future. The notion of bedding the beautiful scribe that had crept into his mind over the last few days shattered into a thousand pieces. That could never happen. It would be an insult to take a woman of such esteemed birth without a marriage agreement, and that could never be for she was not of Viking blood. What would the Caliph think if he discovered that she'd slept in the handmaiden's hut and had worked in the gardens?

"I apologize for Leif's insolence, Princess, and the insult to your family," Siv said.

By the gods, what had she been thinking? He threw Samara a chiding look that promised they would have words about her deceit.

She lowered her lashes as though to hide her shame, but her mouth remained firmly shut.

As his temper eased he recognized it for what it really was, disappointment that she had not trusted him enough to tell him. Disappointment that after all they had shared and his attempts to protect her, she still thought it safer to hide behind a fragile secret and risk abduction than tell him the truth. He stepped away from her and turned his attention to the one problem in the room he could fix.

"You will recompense the Princess for her suffering," he said, unable to keep the anger from his voice.

Siv nodded immediately. "It will be done. In return I ask that you spare my brother's life."

He bristled. How dare Jarl Gustafsson enter his longhouse and expect a mercy he would never allow within his own! "Nei. He will not escape punishment," he demanded, his voice echoing in the otherwise silent room.

"If you want to keep our alliance then you will let me take him when I leave. You have my word that my clansmen will punish him for the shame he has brought us."

He considered Siv's terms. It rankled him to let Leif go, but

Siv had provided an out that would enable him to maintain the alliance with the Gustafsson clan, something he *had* to consider.

Leif pushed his brother away. "Nei. She is my prize. I captured her."

Samara stepped backward, so close that he could feel the warmth of her body against his side. His body stirred. He liked that the little woman sought the safety of his presence. His patience was spent—he wanted this over so he could get Samara alone and question her further. He deserved answers from the princess and he intended to get them.

"Silence," he roared, and glared at Leif with murderous intent. Then he nodded at Siv. "Take him. If he returns he will die."

He felt the moment Samara exhaled beside him, and then began edging toward the door. He couldn't blame her for wanting to escape.

"I want my prize," Leif yelled. "She is mine."

By the gods, the man was asking for another beating. He almost grabbed the finger Leif was pointing at Samara and snapped it in two.

"Control him, Siv, or I'll take my payment in flesh."

"Shut it, brother. You have caused enough trouble." Satisfied his brother would heed his warning, Siv turned back to face Valen with a look of apology. "He'll never sail again."

Leif tensed, rage flashing in his eyes.

Valen nodded his satisfaction with the terms. There was no greater punishment than taking away a Viking's freedom to sail the seas. Leif would live out his days far from here, unable to cause further trouble.

"You will die." Leif attacked, his roar low and guttural like a feral animal caught in a snare as he grabbed Samara around the waist and took her to the ground, their bodies hitting the compacted earth of the longhouse floor with a heavy thud.

A low garbled scream escaped her lips as Leif wrapped a hand around her exposed neck and squeezed.

Nei! He lunged forward. He'd kill the bastard.

Samara's eyes widened, her small hands frantically scratching at Leif's fingers, trying to tear them away.

"I'll never let you go," Leif screamed.

He leapt onto Leif's back, wrapped an arm around his neck, and tumbled to the floor, taking Leif with him. He slid his dagger from the sheath at his waist, his eyes never leaving Samara as he lay beneath the giant bucking man. Was she hurt?

She lay curled on her side, her eyes wide and locked on him. Her chest heaved as she desperately sucked air into her lungs, her fingers covering the red marks on her neck.

Leif clawed at his forearm, drawing blood in his desperation to remove the limb crushing his airway.

The man was at his mercy—one twist and Leif would be dead. Or he could just hold him like this until he ran out of air. Should he do it? A shiver crept up his spine as he realized the truth. Leif was crazed and he would never stop hunting and tormenting Samara.

"She is mine," he hissed in the man's ear.

"Valen, it will be done."

He looked up at Siv Gustafsson, noting the man's eyes were now filled with sorrow and resignation. Even Siv knew this needed to stop, *now*, or Samara would live the rest of her life in fear.

"It will be done," the man repeated.

He nodded once and released Leif from his grasp. Siv was a man of honor—he would keep his word.

Leif rose to his knees, gasping for air, and then took his brother's outstretched hand.

Siv pulled him to his feet. "Brother," he said, and then in one fluid motion, yanked him forward into his embrace.

Leif's eyes widened in shock, and a keening moan fell from his lips as Siv's sword thrust deep into his chest.

Samara gasped as she looked up at them in wide-eyed shock.

"You left me no choice, brother," Siv whispered, and held Leif upright as the lifeblood drained from his body.

Valen rose to his feet and helped Siv lay the lifeless body on the floor. He wanted to offer condolences, yet he could not find the right words. What did one say to someone that had just killed their own brother?

"It is a shame you will not see him in Valhalla."

"Nei." Siv shook his head, his eyes fixed on his brother's corpse. "I loved him because he was my brother, but he had long been touched by madness. He was a coward that preyed on the weak. He does not deserve Óðinn's honor."

"Nevertheless friend, I am sorry for your loss." He patted Siv on the back. He would do whatever he could to ease his burden, starting with removing the body from his longhouse. He turned and motioned Ivvàr over. "Take the body to the Gustafsson ship so it can be prepared for the burning."

Ivvàr nodded and motioned two warriors forward to assist with the task.

"Get back to work," he ordered those that remained, and then bent and scooped Samara up from where she sat trembling on the floor.

She uttered no protest as he carried her out the door and across the lawn toward her room.

Why had he said she was his? He could only hope that none but she had heard his words. It was a foolish mistake uttered in the heat of the moment. Now that he knew who she was, he could never have her. His duty to his clan would not allow it.

She slid her arms up around his neck and burrowed her ashen face into his chest.

By the gods, she felt good in his arms. He couldn't help but wonder what games the gods were playing with him. She couldn't be his bride, yet the fates had sent her for a reason. Mayhap she was a blessing of fortune for his clan? The Caliph would surely come to collect his daughter, providing the opportunity to discuss trade.

He kicked the door to her bedchamber open, turned sideways to enter the small room, and lowered her to stand on her feet.

"Are you well?" he asked, inspecting the darkening flesh on her neck.

She swayed in front of him and brushed her tangled hair from her face. "I will be, just some bruising."

He slammed the door closed behind him and ran a hand through his beard. He winced as he looked around the sparse room with just a bed, an old table, and chair, and a small arched window. It was far from a royal bedchamber.

"Why didn't you tell me, Samara?"

She shook her head.

"Why did you not tell me you are a princess?"

She pressed her lips together, refusing to talk.

She was mistaken if she thought she could deny him—he would have answers. She was a princess, she knew that he deserved an explanation and indeed could demand one. Yet he didn't want to force her, he wanted her to give it to him willingly.

"Samara," he said softly, in the same tone he used to cajole his nieces into relinquishing a favored plaything. "What else are you hiding, Princess? If I am to have any hope of keeping you safe, you need to tell me."

She put her hands on her hips. Her eyes narrowed. "I am not daft. I know I am a prize to any Jarl in these lands. You think you can bend me to your will. I bend to no man."

His nostrils flared. The woman was infuriating. Her own stubbornness could get her killed, or one of his clansmen. He could not allow that. He curled a hand into a fist and beat it on his chest. "I. Am. Jarl. I must know the truth to rule."

She stepped forward, her furious gaze meeting his own and her finger poking him in chest. "You know who I am, that is enough. My reasons why will stay my own."

He drew in a slow steady breath. "You *will* tell me," he said, and advanced.

She retreated, until she was pressed against the stone wall and his hands rested either side of her head, boxing her in.

"Tell me," he said gruffly.

She ducked under his arm and moved out of his reach. "I will *not*, you overbearing donkey's ass." She crossed her arms over her chest and glared at him, looking every bit like a royal princess.

He couldn't believe he hadn't seen through her disguise before. Demands were not going to work. It was clear he couldn't force her to his will. In truth, she was only demanding from him the respect that was rightfully hers as the Caliph's daughter.

He sucked in a slow steady breath and stepped back. "Let me explain."

"Yes?" She arched a dark eyebrow.

"By hiding who you are from me, you put my clan and yourself at great risk. If Leif had attempted to recapture you, my people could have been hurt. It is my duty to protect everybody on this isle and you denied me information I needed to do that. If I'd known that you may still be a target, then I would have increased our defences."

Her arms fell to her sides and she looked a little shamefaced. "I never thought my secret would put your clan at risk. I was afraid. I had just watched all of my people murdered by a Viking."

He was shocked. He'd known she did not trust him, but it

pained him that she thought he would harm her. He backed her against the wall and caged her within his arms again.

"You thought I would hurt you? Have I not cared for you? Is this why you lied to me?"

Her expression went blank. "It was not exactly a lie. I am a scribe, and I have worked with my father for many years in his court."

"Samara..." he growled. He shifted his hands down the wall, reminding her that he had her cornered. Heat built in his body at the sensation of having her so close. This time he wouldn't let her escape until he got some answers. "Why?"

Her throat bobbed as she swallowed hard and touched her neck where Leif had choked her. "Leif targeted me because I was a princess. If one Viking thought to force me to wed for advantage, then what reason would I have to believe that other Vikings wouldn't do the same?"

He trailed a finger across the bruising beginning to darken her skin. "I would never do that," he whispered softly. He could feel the hammering of her pulse beneath his fingertips and heard her breath catch at his touch. "Leif was a man obsessed with violence and inflicting pain. I hate to think of what could have happened if you had not escaped."

She lifted her head defiantly. "I would have lived."

He smiled gently and nodded. "Já, but Leif would have used you until you broke."

She swallowed hard and looked away, her voice shaky as she spoke. "I thought I needed to hide to survive."

He slid his hand under her chin and turned it until she looked at him. "I know. You did what you must. You are strong."

Her bottom lip trembled.

An unfamiliar tenderness swelled within him, a long forgotten sensation that he'd thought lost when Kalda died. "I'll never hurt you, Samara."

"How am I to believe that?" she asked, her eyes blazing with blatant challenge.

"I'll show you." She had a kind heart, a quiet strength, and the face of a goddess. It was no wonder his young warriors followed her around with hungry eyes. She was an irresistible combination of fire and beauty.

The air crackled between them.

He knew he shouldn't, but he wanted to reach out and trace his thumb across her mouth. Those lips... He wanted to caress them, taste them, plunder them.

She placed her hand over his thundering chest, her eyes following the slow descent of his mouth.

Would she let him kiss her? Or push him away?

He inhaled the scent of fresh cut thyme on her skin. Intoxicating. He was hard as steel, his body alive with anticipation. He brushed his lips across her cheek lightly.

She shivered at the gentle touch.

He paused, his lips hovering just beyond hers. Did she want him? He'd shown her what he wanted, but the decision would be hers. His pulse jumped when her tongue darted out and slid across her lips, leaving behind a glistening sheen.

She reached for his shirt, twisting the fabric in her hand and pulling him forward.

He felt a surge of triumph as their bodies met, his hard, hers soft. He wrapped her in his arms and covered her mouth with his. She was as sweet as he'd imagined. He swirled his tongue in a sensual dance that coaxed her to open further for him.

She wrapped her arms around his neck and pressed closer as she let him in. A soft moan, almost like a cat's purr, rumbled in her throat as she met his hungry thrusts and slid her hands up into his hair.

Satisfaction filled him at her reaction and a crack formed in the walls he'd built around his heart the day Kalda was murdered. His love for Kalda remained, but it was bittersweet, dulled by time and buried beneath the weight of his duty and his fear of losing another to the gods. But Samara had survived. She was here, in his arms. The realization that she deemed him worthy of her trust, crumbled the hardened walls, allowing a gentle light to warm his heart.

"Valen," she whispered when they broke apart briefly, her fingers tugging on his hair to pull his mouth down to hers once more.

The sweet taste of her lips drove him wild. His cock throbbed as his hands caressed her slender curves and the swell of her breasts pressed against his chest. When she didn't protest, he cupped the firm flesh in his hand and swiped a thumb across the fabric covering her nipple. By the gods, he needed to lose himself in her and feel her thighs wrapped around him.

She arched her back as he trailed kisses up the curve of her neck, his lips gentling against the bruises forming there.

He needed more. He wanted his mouth to discover all of the places that drove her wild with lust, and hear her cries as he sucked and nipped at those tender places until she begged for release.

The sharp peal of women's laughter rang out beyond the door and then disappeared as they continued down the hall.

He lifted his lips from her neck. Slowly, the fog of lust ebbed and he found himself in Samara's small bedchamber with her flushed body in his arms and his loins aching for release. What was he doing? He was Jarl—he couldn't do this. He released her and stepped back abruptly.

Her eyes fluttered open, slightly glazed for a few moments before she registered the distance between them, and then they rose to meet his.

He had to say it. "I should not have done that."

She paused a moment, and then cocked her head and shrugged. "It takes two for a kiss. I don't recall fighting you off."

A throat cleared in the doorway.

He glanced over his shoulder. Ásta stood waiting with a pitcher of steaming water in her hands. How much had she seen? He hadn't even heard her open the door.

He turned back to Samara. "We will talk later."

She lowered and raised her head, an act he recognized as polite dismissal.

What had he been thinking kissing a princess? He deserved a smack to the back of his head for his stupidity. He walked to the door and paused beside Ásta.

"Take care of her," he commanded, and then left, each step he took replacing stones as he started to rebuild the crumbled wall around his heart.

"A mistake," he muttered to himself as he stormed toward the river. He shook his head. He'd made a terrible mistake. Now that he'd tasted her, he'd never be able to stay away.

CHAPTER EIGHT

SAMARA

*S*amara sat in the shade, high on the bank of the river, and watched the Vikings swim in the river below. Their laughter drifted on the gentle breeze, reminding her of the children that played in the river Tigris beyond the palace wall. The whole clan seemed to have stopped work to escape the midday heat in the cooling waters.

She plucked a piece of grass and rolled it between her fingers. She'd been surprised when Valen had invited her to join the outing at the morning meal. She'd seen so little of him the last four days that it was obvious that he regretted their kiss. It hurt that he could shun her with such ease, whilst she struggled to banish him from her thoughts.

Two leather boots stopped in front of her, blocking her view of the swimmers.

The hair on her arms stood on end, and she knew that the long legs encased in tight pants that hugged a pair of hard muscular thighs were attached to the man who had invaded her thoughts.

Valen bent one knee to the ground and rested his forearms on his other knee. "Well met, Samara."

His intense blue eyes reminded her of lure the puff adder used to attract prey. She'd lose herself in those sapphire pools if she weren't careful.

"Jarl Eriksson." She nodded in greeting.

He tucked a lock of sunlit hair that hung across his eyes behind his ears. "Aren't you going to swim?"

She shook her head. "I cannot," she lied. Her father would never forgive her. The carefree Viking ways were nothing like the guarded reserve of life at the palace. She'd almost fainted when everybody had discarded their clothing haphazardly and run into the water naked.

He tilted his head. "You cannot swim?"

Unable to bear the intensity of his gaze, she looked around him at the sandy shore and the clear green water flowing around mossy boulders. She ached to feel its cooling touch on her skin, to dip below the surface and lose herself in the underwater world or float on the surface watching the clouds. She was used to denying herself to adhere to the expectations of her royal position, but this time it stung a lot. How would it feel to live without restrictions? She longed for the freedom these Vikings took for granted.

"Swimming is forbidden."

He grunted a laugh. "Forbidden by whom? I am Jarl here, and I say swimming is not forbidden. I can see that you want to. Why do you refuse?"

She should have known he'd see through her. Valen was far too observant to fall for her half-hearted deflection.

"My father would be furious. Here nobody seems to notice bare flesh, but modesty is closely guarded in my world." A princess that broke with tradition would encourage others to flout the rules. She couldn't do it.

"Ahh, but your father is not here. He would never know." Valen's eyes twinkled, his mouth curving into a playful grin.

A flush of heat spread across her skin. She willed her face

into the indifferent mask that she wielded like a sword on her enemies at court. "Why are you doing this, Valen? You ended that kiss, and then ignored me. Why are you crossing the limits that *you* set?"

His expression hardened. He pushed himself upright and ran a hand through his hair.

She looked up at him, taking in the muscles rippling under his white shirt as he moved.

His jaw flexed as his gaze returned to hers. "You play the distant princess, but I see you. I've watched you teaching the children numbers in the sand on the beach, and discussing plants with our healer. You're unlike any other woman I've known. I want to know more about you."

"You do?" Her heart skipped a beat. He'd been watching her even when they were apart. This tough Viking had seen straight through to the heart of her, the place she kept hidden.

"I..." He paused as though reluctant to continue. "I can't stay away anymore."

She saw how hard that was for him to admit. She liked that he trusted her enough to show his softer side too. "I don't want you to stay away." She held his gaze. "I feel this pull between us too, but..."

His eyes darkened to the mesmerizing hue of the blue flame of a fire on a cold winter's night. "It's not wise." He turned toward the swimmers in the river.

She was torn—it was hard to break a lifetime of living by the rules, but she could feel him retreating again. She couldn't let that happen. She was new to such things, but she wanted him as she had never wanted a man before. It was confusing, terrifying, and undeniable. She yearned to feel as carefree and independent as his people did, even just for a short while, and he could give it to her. Undoubtedly, she'd spent too long with these Vikings, because before she knew it she had spoken.

"All I have ever done is learn and fulfil my duty to my people. Always guarded, always watched. It is suffocating."

His smouldering gaze snapped back to her. "I know that feeling well."

A moment of understanding passed between them. Regardless of all of their differences, the heavy burden that came with leadership was something they had in common.

"Já. I guess you do. I would cry when my tutors refused to allow me to play with the children. I even envied the hunting hawks, for at least they were untethered occasionally and free to soar. I need to know what that freedom feels like, Valen."

"What are you saying?"

"We should take the few moments we have together."

"I'll not bed you, Samara." His voice was a low rumbling growl that made her shiver. "You're a princess, and must remain untouched."

She swallowed hard. "I'm not suggesting *that*." She glanced away so he wouldn't see the flush of heat on her skin.

"What are you suggesting?"

She summoned the courage to face him. If she was going to do this, he needed to see that she was steadfast in her decision.

"I will leave here soon. Until then, I want you to show me how to live like a Viking. I want to follow my own path just once, before I must marry the man my father chooses." She held her breath. Would he push her away again?

"Samara—"

She interrupted before he could reject her proposal. "You know how it feels to be weighed down by duty, Valen. I think you need some enjoyment in your life too."

He moved in front of her, blocking the sun with his large frame. "I will agree, if you agree not to hide anything else from me."

She smiled and nodded, surprised that he had capitulated so easily. "I promise. No more secrets."

"Can you swim as well as you negotiate, Princess?"

Her eyes widened at his teasing question. How had he known she could swim?

He rocked back on his heels and grinned down at her. "What? I know you're not the proper princess you make out to be."

She straightened her back and raised her nose in the air. "I'll have you know that I am a proper princess." She grinned, letting mirth flicker in her eyes.

"Careful, princess, you cannot lie, remember?" His lips twitched in the corner and his eyes sparkled with amusement.

"Did you really think I wouldn't notice that you never said you cannot swim, just that it was forbidden?" He stepped forward, so close that she had to tilt her head right back to look at him.

"I notice *everything* about you."

His words caused a strange fluttering sensation in her stomach. Had he noticed her eyes following him? Or how she couldn't breathe when he touched her? She looked down to hide the heated flush on her face at the thought that he could read her so easily. She shrugged, pretending nonchalance. "I may have snuck out of the palace to swim in the Tigris River while the city slept."

His burst of deep laughter made her smile. She looked up at his strong jaw and striking face. "I've never told anyone that," she admitted.

"I knew you were trouble, Princess." He extended his hand toward her. "Come. There's a place upstream where we can swim alone. Nobody will ever know."

She slid her fingers into his rough calloused palm, wondering why she felt like she was jumping into the deep, unable to see the bottom. She focused on the sand that oozed between her bare toes as Valen led her along the riverbank. Goodness, what was she doing? Was this a mistake?

He stopped around a bend in the river where a rush of rapids flowed into a wide pool before meandering more slowly downstream to where the clan frolicked. Then he dropped her hand, grabbed the bottom of his shirt, and pulled it over his head.

All air rushed from her lungs. She couldn't tear her eyes from his body. His hairless chest was an expanse of golden skin that shimmered in the dappled light of the overhanging trees. Her fingers itched to trace across it and linger over the inked markings that wrapped around his muscular arms.

He turned from her, slid off his boots and breeches, and then walked down to the water.

Her breath caught and she hastily averted her eyes, but they soon returned to roam the long lean lines of his limbs, his thick powerful thighs, and the firm globes of his ass. Her body hummed in response. He looked just like the rendering of the Viking god Óðinn carved into the pillars in the great hall.

He paused and looked over his shoulder at her. "I'll race you to the other side."

She laughed as he waded into the water.

"Come, Princess. You're the one that wanted to live like a Viking." He turned to face her, the clear water lapping at the hard ridges of his stomach that led downward and disappeared below the surface.

A sense of urgency drove her forward. This was it, the moment she'd always wanted, the moment that those midnight adventures to swim in the Tigris never quite satisfied. This was her chance to experience life beyond the rules and expectations of others. She forced her trembling fingers to unbutton the front of her dress. Could she do it? She straightened her back and pulled her dress off. As it fell to her feet with a soft swoosh, she wrapped an arm across her breasts and shielded between her legs where she knew he would be able to see beneath the thin fabric of her shift.

"Já. It is as I imagined, your skin is the color of honey all over," Valen said, his hungry eyes roaming her body.

A rush of warmth flooded her, the admiration in his eyes creating a delicious throbbing between her legs.

"You needn't hide yourself from me."

She summoned her courage, lifted her chin, and dropped her arms. If she was going to do this, she needed to do it as the Viking did.

Unbridled fervor blazed in his eyes as she slowly walked to water's edge.

The cool water lapping at her bare feet reminded her that she was about to swim naked with a man...alone. She looked up at the clouds, savoring the warmth of the sunlight on her face and the cool water caressing her legs as she waded into the river, her fingertips trailing across the surface.

"Are you going to let me win?" He splashed water at her, and then dove beneath the surface, giving her a brief glimpse of his toned buttocks.

Joyful laughter broke free from her chest, where it had been caged for years awaiting release. She dove in, determined to show him that she was serious about winning. She reveled in the smooth rhythmic strokes as she pushed herself harder and faster than she'd ever swum, but the current was strong and she knew she'd never catch him. She broke the surface and grinned, her whole body alive with exhilaration.

He leaned back against a boulder, the water lapping at his waist, his wet hair hanging loose over his shoulders, and trails of water dripping down his chest.

"Let's do it again." She wanted more.

He crossed his arms and looked down at her, his lips twitching. "You sure? I won." His teasing tone held the arrogance of a winner.

She squeezed the water from her hair. "You cheated." She pushed him playfully in the shoulder.

"Nei." He reached for her hand and tugged. When she stumbled forward, his other arm slid around her waist to press her closer.

She swallowed hard, and raised her eyes to find him watching her.

"I played to win."

A warm flush crept into her cheeks. A hard muscular thigh slid between her legs and pressed against where she ached. Her breath quickened. She needed to touch him, needed to satisfy those cravings that had left her needy and sleepless since their kiss. She trailed her fingertips over the hard planes of his chest, noting how he shuddered when they skimmed across his nipples.

"You know it wasn't a fair race, Valen."

His gaze darkened and she glimpsed the dangerous warrior lurking within him. "I never said I'd play fair. I always get what I want."

She shivered. He was not talking about swimming anymore. He was looking at her as if she was a sweet treat to be devoured. "What do you want?" Her breathy whisper matched the fluttering of her heart.

His eyes flared as she bit down on her bottom lip. "You," he groaned.

She licked her lips, every second feeling stretched out as his gaze followed the wet slide of her tongue.

His jaw clenched.

He was fighting for restraint—she couldn't let him stop, not now. She stroked the lines of his shoulders, pressing her breasts against his chest. She could feel his heartbeat, its furious pace matching her own.

His whole body was tense against hers. He was holding back.

She didn't want that. She wanted him to lose control, to show her all of him, even the parts he kept hidden. She knew he would not hurt her, not even if he lost control. She pushed up onto her toes until her mouth hovered close to his, and looked into his eyes so he would know she was certain.

"Take me, Valen," she whispered.

"I shouldn't, but I can't help myself." He crushed his mouth to hers, the fervent strokes of his tongue stoking the fire deep within her into an inferno.

She wrapped her arms around his neck and everything disappeared. The rough touch of the boulder against her arm, the gentle trickle of the river, even the daylight. There was only the taste of his mouth and the heat pooling between her legs. She moaned and pressed closer, feeling the hard ridge of his desire pressed against her stomach.

He pulled away, a low guttural groan indicating his reluctance. "We should stop."

Still dazed, Samara fingered her swollen lips. "Swimming... kissing. I like these Viking ways. What else will you show me?"

"Pleasing things," he whispered in her ear, his hot breath hitting her neck and making her shudder.

"Like what?" she stammered, her eyes drifting closed.

His teeth scraped across her earlobe, before his tongue darted out to soothe the tender flesh.

Oh my! She wanted...more. She didn't know what was missing, but she was sure Valen could give it to her.

"Like fishing ..." His lips burned a trail down her neck. "Or hawking. And kissing... much more kissing."

"Hawking?" Samara's eyes popped open. She'd long wanted to try hawking, but no matter how much she'd begged her father, his hawking parties had always left without her.

"Have you been?" Valen asked, as he nipped at her neck.

She gasped at the surge of pleasure that followed the sting of his gentle bite. "It is forbidden."

He pulled back and looked down at her. "Naught is forbidden here, Princess. I'll find time to take you."

She whimpered at the friction of her nipples rubbing against his chest and the press of his hardened staff against her belly, and then abandoned all coherent thought as his hands gently cupped her face and he claimed her mouth once more.

CHAPTER NINE

VALEN

*V*alen swallowed a groan as he kissed Samara long
and deep. She tasted like the sweet fresh water and
his thirst was unquenchable.

She whimpered her approval, and her lips moved with the
same ardent desperation as his own.

He pulled away, his gaze dropping to the wet shift plastered
to where her breasts pressed to his chest, creating a tantalizing
swell of creamy flesh. He trailed soft kisses down to the hollow
of her neck. Blessed Freya, help him. He was painfully hard.
Holding her in his arms was foolish—she made him feel more
alive than he had in years. He'd long avoided contact with
women, beyond occasional rutting to satiate his urges, content
to perform the act without intimacy or attachment. But this,
holding Samara against him, threatened to equal what he'd felt
with Kalda.

"Valen..." she said in a breathy whisper.

He needed to stop now, or he'd wrap her legs around his
waist and take her until she screamed his name as she tightened
around him. He shivered. By the gods, it was hopeless—he
couldn't control this hunger for her.

"NEI! Calla, my baby!" The piercing scream cut through the soothing trickle of water flowing past and birds chirping.

He snapped his head up, instantly pulled from the intoxicating haze of rapture. He knew that voice—it was Mara.

Samara shoved him away and listened attentively to the murmur of panicked shouts drifting on the breeze. "Something's wrong." She dove in and swam away from him, her arms cutting through the water swiftly as she crossed the river.

He followed and chased her up the riverbank to their discarded clothes.

She grabbed her dress and threw it on, oblivious to the fact her wet shift clung to her skin, baring all. "Hurry!" She ran along the riverbank toward the noise.

Were they under attack? Valen yanked on his boots and rushed after her. He had to keep her close, where he could protect her, until he could assess the threat. "Samara, wait."

She ignored him and disappeared around the bend that had sheltered them from view.

He ran faster and caught up to Samara as she pushed her way through to the front of a panicked crowd that had gathered at the water's edge.

"La..." Samara's hands flew to her chest.

"Nei!"

His gaze fell to where his clanswoman Mara sat on the damp riverbank with her little girl lying limp in her arms. The child's skin was drained of color, her lips the same dangerous tinge of blue he'd seen on many a drowned warrior.

"How did this happen?"

"The children were jumping from a tree into the river. She must have hit her head, because she was found floating face down," Dànel said.

"Wake up, Calla. Wake up," Mara sobbed, as she rocked her lifeless daughter back and forth.

He crouched down, his heart sinking as he watched Mara

wrestle with her grief. The child wasn't breathing—it was too late.

Samara dropped to her knees in front of Mara.

He thought she would offer the woman comfort, but she reached out, gently smoothed the child's hair from her eyes, and then bent to listen over the child's mouth.

Mara shoved her hard in the shoulder. "Get away. Get away from her." The woman's eyes were wide with terror as she screeched and pulled her child away.

Samara teetered off balance but then leaned toward Mara once more. "Let me try save her," she pleaded. She lifted her eyes to meet his. "Let me try," she repeated.

He paused. Should he let her try? Something in her pleading eyes gave him a spark of hope. He would do anything for the little girl to live. He looked at Mara. "Let her try."

Mara collapsed as though all will to live abandoned her as he and Samara pried the child from her arms and laid her flat on the ground.

He looked up at Samara, taking in her stern-faced expression and pursed lips. "What can I do?" he asked.

Samara released a shaky breath. "Keep everyone back. I must do this alone."

He nodded, and pushed himself to his feet. "Move away." He spread his arms wide and forced everyone back.

He stood behind her, prepared to step in if the crowd turned on her. If she failed, the whispers of her being a witch would be unstoppable. He could only hope it would not come to that.

Samara pinched Calla's tiny nose between her thumb and forefinger and used her other hand to open her little mouth. She bent at the waist, opened her mouth, and placed it over the child's open one.

He jerked. Was she kissing the dead child? Did she want to get herself killed?

Shock rippled through the crowd.

He raised his hand to still the few that had stepped forward prepared to defend the small child.

Samara's chest heaved as she exhaled with a noisy whoosh.

Calla's tiny chest rose as it filled with air, and then fell as Samara moved her mouth away.

He watched in fascination as she repeated the action. She was plainly trying to breathe life in the dead child. Would it work?

Her hands shook as the powerful force he'd felt many times on the battlefield rushed through her body, but not once did her focus waver from the child as she repeated the act over and over. A fierce woman hid beneath her reserved exterior, one that would do anything to save the child.

Though time had slowed to a crawl, as it often did when faced with death, eventually he knew that the child had been dead far too long. Samara had tried, but failed to save the girl.

"Breathe, little one." He watched as Samara, oblivious to the watchful crowd and passing of time, continued to force air into the lifeless child, unwilling to accept the death in front of her.

He couldn't let this continue any longer. The gods had claimed the child. He crouched down beside Samara. He placed a hand on her shoulder and realized that her whole body shook beneath her damp dress. She needed to stop before she made herself sick.

"Samara…"

Her shoulder tensed beneath his hand.

"She's…"

As he spoke, the little girl's stomach contracted, her legs pulling up toward her chest, then falling back to the ground.

His heart skipped a beat.

Mara gasped, her teary eyes still riveted on her daughter's body.

Calla's body jerked once more, and her scrawny shoulders rose and fell as water began to spill from her mouth.

He froze, the pounding of his heart escalating to a deafening roar in his ears.

Samara pushed the girl onto her side and thumped her on the back hard three times.

The child spluttered, vomited up more liquid, and then opened her eyes and began to wail.

Thank the gods! The surge of elation was so strong he almost fell back on his ass, just barely saving himself in time. She'd done it! She'd wrestled the child from the clutches of the goddess Hel.

"Calla. Oh, my baby." Mara reached for her child, and then stopped and looked at Samara.

Samara slumped, her shoulders sagging as she nodded that it was safe.

Mara pulled her daughter into her arms, tears running down her face as she hugged her daughter tight.

He wrapped an arm around Samara and lifted her to her feet, noting how she wobbled unsteadily. She was on the downward slide that followed life-threatening battles. He pressed her to his side and held her upright. She was strong and stubborn, but the shaking had spread to her whole body and he knew her legs would not work yet.

She went limp in his arms, allowing him to support her.

His attention returned to his people. He didn't know how they'd react to what they'd just seen. She'd saved the child, so he doubted they'd hurt her, but would they fear her even more? Fear made men unpredictable—he'd seen it often on the battlefield.

The crowd surged forward, their gentle hands reaching out to pat Samara on the back or clasp her trembling fingers in a show of gratitude.

The tension eased from his shoulders. He watched her, tired but politely returning each thankful gesture and smile. Óðinn, he was proud of this woman. She had fought hard, even through his own doubts, to save one of his own. He cupped her chin and tilted her head back.

Her eyes were glassy as she looked through him. She was still dazed, and completely unaware that she had won the heart of his clan. In her haste to save Calla, she had abandoned all pretense and shown everyone the truth of her kind heart. Now that the Eriksson clan had claimed her, she would always have a place with his people.

"I did it." Samara rested her head on his chest, a satisfied smile lighting her face.

"That you did, Princess." He swept an arm under her legs and lifted her up against his chest. As he looked down at her, the first twinge of hope he'd felt in years crept in. She was a princess and his clan had claimed her. Mayhap he could have it all? The very admission pained him, but he still wanted the comfort of a woman's love and all that it entailed—laughter, tender caresses, passionate nights, children...

If he could just convince his father, then mayhap they could merge their two kingdoms, and he could have his feisty princess too?

CHAPTER TEN

VALEN

$\mathcal{F}$our nights later, Valen stood in the great hall beside Rorik and nursed his ale. The room was loud with the chatter of competition, heated debate about rules, and the occasional rowdy accusation of cheating that required he intervene and broker peace. He smiled as he watched his guests play the various games of strategy and skill.

Rorik shook his head at the warriors gathered around a table at the far end of the room, chugging down pitchers of ale. "They are willing to risk tomorrow's pain to be crowned champion drinker. Fools!"

"Já. They shall regret it when I wake them at dawn." His gaze left the rowdy group and moved to watch his brother Ulf move a piece on a Hnefatafl board and nod at Siv Gustafsson opposite him. Hnefatafl was the most popular game by far, and Valen had counted more than six battle boards in play around the hall.

As he found himself doing often these days, he searched the room for Samara. The long forgotten thrill of wooing a woman had returned since that first kiss at the river. That she was forbidden to him had only heightened his hunger for her company.

"Your eyes betray you, brother. Is that where you disappeared this day?" Rorik's teasing tone held a twinge of concern.

"I was hawking," he replied, omitting to mention Samara had accompanied him. She was a natural, not that he was surprised. He'd been jealous of the damn bird, until she'd reminded him of the secret kisses they'd stolen over the last few days. He'd almost thrown her over his shoulder and taken her to his bed when she'd clasped his hand beneath the table earlier tonight. His yearning for the woman was staggering.

"Is that what we are calling it now?" Rorik gave him a knowing look, and then walked off and disappeared out the door, no doubt seeking the solitude of his hut and the company of the livestock he tended.

A few moments later, he spotted Samara across the hall in deep discussion with his mother. He couldn't hold back his grin.

She had her back to him, her dark hair hanging loose with the tips of her dark curls kissing her perfectly rounded ass.

He adjusted the part of him that always swelled when she was near. By the gods, he ached for her as he had for no other woman.

A smile lit his mother's face as she patted Samara affectionately on the shoulder. The days of mistrust before Samara had saved Calla seemed like the distant past. Everyone adored her, especially his family.

Especially him.

"I see you watching her."

He stiffened at the harsh tone in his father's voice.

"Don't do this to yourself." The Jarl's cold stare was intent upon Samara and his wife.

So, Samara hadn't won over *everyone* in his family. Not that there was anything she could do that would make her a suitable match in his father's eyes.

"You see naught, Father."

"Do not lie to me." His father turned to him, his displeasure clear on his face. "No good can come of this for either of you. You must marry for an alliance."

He huffed in response. He loved his father, but the old man was wrong this time. "She's a royal princess, and an alliance with Caliph Radi-el Abbasid would be good for the clan."

"Nei." His father barked the word with a curt finality. "Your wife must be Viking."

"But we could open up new trade routes."

"I said nei. You needn't wed her to trade with the Caliph, but you *must* marry the daughter of a Jarl to secure another Viking ally. You know this, Valen." His father scowled, forbidding further argument, before he turned on his heel and stomped away.

He sighed and rubbed the back of his neck as he watched his father return to the raised chair he would soon occupy as Jarl. The weight of responsibility that settled back on his shoulders felt heavier than ever before. His father was right. He must wed to strengthen his position as Jarl, as not doing so would be seen as weakness and would leave his people and lands open to attack. He couldn't risk it. There was too much at stake to throw away tradition.

"You look vexed. Is something wrong?" The heat of Samara's hand on his shoulder burned straight through his shirt.

He studied the roughly carved rune on the smooth timber cup in his hand. He couldn't have her. He had to make her see that.

"What are we doing, Princess?"

The question was vague, but from her knowing look, she understood his meaning. A soft smile lit her face. "Soon I will be gone. Nothing more than a collection of thoughts that die with those I met on this isle. We will both be alone."

"You will not be lonely." He frowned at the thought of her sad and alone in a palace deep in the desert of her homeland.

"Like you, I will marry a stranger. We will both be lonely, Valen."

She was right. He already lost Kalda and soon he'd have to let Samara go too. He did not want to wake up and not see this strong, brave, and stubborn woman that challenged him in every way. His heart swelled with a feeling he'd thought long since dead. He felt like he'd been struck down by Thor's hammer as the truth hit him—he was falling for her.

She tilted her head and studied him curiously, waiting for him to speak.

He admired this kind-hearted, witty, and often exasperating princess! Somehow, she had laid claim to his barren heart and brought it back to life. She was right—there was a good chance that his marriage would be loveless and lonely, but if the other clans discovered that he had chosen to bed her rather than one of their daughters, then he would never find a wife. And he knew naught of the consequences she would face, but surely they would not be good either.

"We risk too much for something fleeting," he said. She had to understand that.

She shook her head, leaned closer, and lowered her voice. "We will keep it a secret. Soon I will be gone and there will be no danger to your kingdom."

Was she right? He weighed her proposition carefully. If they could keep it a secret, then there would be little harm done. Even so, bedding the forbidden princess was dangerous. He would stop before it went that far.

She rose up onto her toes and whispered in his ear. "I vow to embrace every moment until we must part. Will you?"

Her hot breath on his ear added fuel to the fire that her words had sparked within him. By the gods, he wanted to take every moment they could to be together too.

She lowered her heels to the floor, sipped her wine, and looked around the room casually. Maybe this could work. She was very good at presenting what people expected to see. She had fooled him after all.

"Já. I will." He nodded his acquiescence before he could change his mind. Soon enough he would be Jarl and sacrifice his own happiness for his people. Just this once he would do as he wished, and hope that it would bring him the comfort she spoke of in the years ahead. He would do this, and hope that it didn't kill him to watch her leave.

Her eyes widened as though she was surprised at his easy capitulation.

"Come," he said, and led her to an empty table. "Let's play."

"What is the game?" she asked, her eyes shining as she placed her cup on the table and lowered herself gracefully in the chair opposite him.

"Hnefatafl."

"King's table?" she translated, and leaned forward to study the board.

He nodded. "Do you know it?"

She shook her head. "Nei."

"Good. I will have a chance at besting you again." He winked at her.

"Hmm. Mayhap you can do it this time without cheating." Mirth twinkled in her eyes. "What are the rules?"

~

*T*wo hours later, Valen studied the Hnefatafl board on the table in front of him. The hall had slowly emptied as the inebriated stumbled off to bed leaving behind just a few guests clustered around the tables nearby.

"How did you do that?" he asked, bewildered. She had snuck her pieces through his defences and had his king trapped...again.

She leaned back in her chair and smiled at him serenely. "I can't share my secrets with the enemy," she teased.

He pressed his lips together to halt his smile. He enjoyed the easy banter between them. She had a quick wit and never let his teasing go unchallenged. "But you only learned to play tonight." He shook his head in disbelief.

She shrugged. "I am a quick study. It is very similar to a game we call Shatranj." She sipped her wine, her eyes dancing as she enjoyed his confusion.

Was there anything she couldn't do, or didn't know? "Can I ask you something?"

She nodded. "Anything."

"How did you know what to do at the river with the child?" He'd replayed it repeatedly in his mind, yet he still could not make sense of what had happened that day. Never in all his years had he seen someone return from the dead like that child had.

She paused for a few moments as she weighed her answer, and then traced the rim of her cup with a finger as she spoke. "In my third year of study, I spent a summer assisting a doctor. I learned much from him about setting bones and tending to severe ailments."

"So you learnt how to save Calla from him?"

She nodded. "One day we attended a man who had fallen in the river and could not swim. It was too late to save him, but Doctor Paqui explained how to cover the mouth and breathe. He called it the kiss of life."

"Thank the gods you were at the river that day. The child lives because of you."

She smiled gently. "It does not always work. I was fortunate."

He returned his focus to the board game and made his move, capturing one of her pieces to clear a path for his king to escape. "What other lessons does a princess study?"

She placed her cup beside the board and leaned forward,

resting her hands on the table as she studied her pieces on the board. "Cooking, painting, the stars…"

Watching her lips twitch as her mind worked was sweet torture. He wanted to jump across the table and press his mouth to hers. He downed his ale instead and leaned back, adjusting himself discretely beneath the table. "The stars?"

She lifted a piece between two fingers and then replaced it, tapping her chin thoughtfully as she spoke. "I assisted with mapping the patterns of the stars in the night sky. Others studied the movements of the moon and the sun."

"We navigate our ships by the stars."

She nodded distractedly, and then plucked one of his pieces from the board and quickly replaced it with one of hers. "I win."

"What?" He couldn't hide his shock. *Again?*

She burst into laughter, and then covered her mouth with her hand to stifle the sound. Her shoulders shook as she struggled to control her amusement.

"Did you let a woman beat you again, Valen?" Rúna called out from across the room.

He threw his hands up in defeat. "I'm trying not to. She's too good."

"So you don't want another match?" Samara's lips curled up in the corners as she raised an eyebrow at him.

"Nei. You have punished me enough for one day." He pushed to his feet. This was the time when he usually walked her to her room and kissed her senseless. He couldn't do that now. Tonight he didn't have the strength to resist. If he got her anywhere near a bed he wouldn't stop until she begged him to take her.

She followed silently as he led her away from the hall, skirting around the edge of the village, and then up the steps to the stone tower.

An owl hooted in the distance as he looked out across the shimmering waves that gently caressed the shore and steeled himself to face her. "I'll not walk you to your room tonight."

She tilted her head, confused. "Why?"

He didn't know how it was possible, but she looked even more beautiful in the dark with just the crescent moon and the stars of the night sky lighting her from behind. His cock hardened.

"It's too dangerous, Samara. Each day it gets harder to stop at just a kiss. I can't give you more." He couldn't bed her, no matter how much his body ached for her. A royal princess must remain untouched for her husband. He'd not take her innocence and ruin her chance for future happiness.

She looked at him from beneath hooded eyes as she closed the distance between them. She smiled as she pressed her body into his and curled her arms up around his neck.

"I don't believe you'd deny me anything," she whispered.

He swallowed hard.

Her soft lips parted and her throaty whisper broke the final threads of his restraint.

"Kiss me."

By Óðinn, she tempted him as no other had. He wrapped her in his arms and claimed her mouth. She tasted of the rich oaky tang of wine. It drove him wild. She drove him wild. She could bring even the gods to their knees. He was defenceless against her.

She gripped his hair in her hands and took over the kiss, biting his lower lip before her tongue delved inside in a desperate, savage invasion. She consumed him like a wildfire, and he loved it. Then she crawled up his body and wrapped her legs around his waist, the soft mound of her womanhood pressed against the silky steel that was so eager to find a way inside her.

He stumbled back to the low stone wall and sat down with her straddling his thighs. She was right—he could deny her nothing. He flicked open the buttons of her dress and pushed it down. A quick tug of the laces and her shift fell open to reveal her firm bronzed breasts that hung heavy in his hands.

"Beautiful..." he whispered reverently. He dipped his head and kissed her neck. When she moaned softly, he continued nipping and sucking a trail downward.

She gasped sharply as he sucked a tender nipple into his hot mouth.

He couldn't take his eyes off her as she closed her eyes and succumbed to the pleasure. She was magnificent. Even the goddess Freya would walk in the shadow of her beauty.

A surge of warmth wrapped around his heart and latched on as she surrendered and trusted him with her body. He slid a hand up under her dress and pushed fabric to the side, seeking the source of pleasure that he knew would push her over the edge. He could give her that bliss, he had to—he couldn't let her go without feeling her shatter in his arms just once.

She moaned as his thumb found that place. Her hips rocked forward, brushing her core along the length of his throbbing cock as she sought the pressure of his touch.

He gave her what she needed, guiding her hips into a sensual rhythm as his fingers pushed her to the brink. She was almost there. He watched her mouth fall open, etching that final fleeting moment before she crested in his mind forever, before he grazed her nipple with his teeth and sucked hard on the furled bud.

Her back arched, and her arms fell from around his neck. She looked magnificent with the dim moonlight lighting her upturned face, her long hair falling in dark waves down behind her.

Her soft hair caressed his thighs, adding to the sensual, captivating experience of pleasuring her. His arm tightened around her waist as he thrust his fingers inside her warmth.

"Let go. I have you."

Her body stiffened as she cried out, and then she soared, her body shuddering with the force of her release.

He ignored the throbbing staff in his breeches and held her

in his arms as the aftershocks wracked her body. When her breathing slowed, he placed her on her feet and fastened her dress. He'd never regret what had just happened, but he could not take it any further.

"It's time for bed, Samara."

She swayed unsteadily as her head bobbed.

He memorized the languid contented smile on her face, his chest swelling with pride. He'd caused that drunken daze of satisfaction. He looked away so that he would not succumb to the temptation to reach for her and never let go.

"Go now, Samara."

CHAPTER ELEVEN

SAMARA

*S*amara pushed her bedchamber door closed and fell against it with a contented sigh. In Valen's embrace, she'd felt more alive than she ever had before. Even now, the rush of warmth that had chased away the aftermath of his touch left her feeling as if she could cross the desert barefoot. Oh, how his hands made her body sing. She wanted more.

"I know that look."

She gasped at the soft voice coming from the shadows. Who was it?

Ásta walked into the light of the smouldering fire in the corner of the room and picked up the folded nightshirton the end of the bed.

"You scared me." She stepped away from the door, her fear disappearing. It was only Ásta.

Her friend gave her a knowing smile. "I saw you leave with Valen and thought you might have need of me."

There was no hiding anything from the clever handmaiden. She grinned back, letting the joy on her face betray her. She'd been caught, and she didn't even care. Over the last week Ásta had become a loyal friend and confidant. She knew she could rely on her discretion.

"We took a walk," she said, and crossed the room and sat down on the chair to remove her boots.

Ásta walked up behind her. "Hmm...I bet it was quite the journey."

"It was...nice." She stood so that Ásta could help remove her dress, the sensual caress of the fabric sliding upward reminding her of Valen's heated touch. Those fingers, those hands...

"I'd say from the rosy glow to your skin that it was more than nice." Ásta laid the dress on the wooden chair in the corner of the small room and picked up the carved bone comb. "Sit and I shall braid your hair."

Samara spun around. "I saw you returning to the hall, Ásta. Now that I think about it, Valen's friend, Dànel, disappeared at the same time you did." She raised an eyebrow. She had questions for her curious friend too!

A pink flush crept across Ásta's pale skin. "I...it is naught," she said, waving her hand dismissively.

She scoffed at the obvious lie and shook her head. "I do not believe that. You would not give yourself without affection. There is something between you two."

Now that she thought about it, Ásta had returned to the hall alone, only to flee a short while later from a darkhaired man after what appeared to be a tense exchange. Whoever the man was, he was powerful, and she knew well the liberties his kind thought they could take from defenceless handmaidens. Had he propositioned her? Men like that often thought they could take what was not offered. She'd not allow that to be Ásta's fate.

"Who was the man that you fled from?"

Ásta's eyes widened and the color drained from her face. "He is nobody."

That lie was even worse than her first. Ásta looked as terrified as someone who had seen a djinn, a shape shifting spirit.

"If he has hurt you..."

Ásta grabbed her hand and cradled it in her own. The amber hair that flowed down over her shoulders and back to her waist, danced back and forth as she shook her head.

"He is merely a shadow from the past that I'd rather forget. Promise me you'll not mention this to anyone." It was painful watching her friend pretend all was well when it was obvious that the man terrified her, but clearly, Ásta's need for secrecy was truth.

"Very well, I will keep your secret, if you will keep mine." She would honor Ásta's request, but watch vigilantly for any signs of mistreatment and report them to Valen or Rúna. Suddenly weary, she sat down on the sleeping furs draped over her bed.

"My lips are sealed." Ásta settled on her knees behind her. "Now, tell me of Valen."

The teeth of the comb pressed into her back as Ásta started at her waist, and then moved upward, tugging it through her messed hair.

"He makes me feel..." She released a wistful sigh. Valen made her feel hot, bothered, and confused. Their stolen kisses and being in his arms felt wonderful, but when they were apart there was an emptiness inside her that made no sense.

"I understand," Ásta said softly.

"You do?"

"Já. It is a blessing to share a great love..." Ásta's voice trailed off as her fingers deftly weaved Samara's hair into a braid.

Love? Did she love Valen? Was that what this was? This undeniable need to be close to him, to watch him work, and observe his kind, yet firm, leadership with his people. Could it explain her overwhelming hunger to feel his touch, and the heat that built within her under his skilful hands? She shuddered in delight at the mere memory.

Ásta released a long wistful sigh.

Samara understood exactly how her friend was feeling. Then

there was this ever-present dull ache when she was apart from Valen. Everything else she felt she could justify as admiration and desire of the flesh, but that dull ache, that *did* feel remarkably like her heart yearning for its beloved. The harder she tried to deny the thought the more it persisted. Valen was her beloved. The truth filled her with a stunning clarity—it had crept up on her slowly, admiration, trust, friendship, and then love. She loved him!

"A blessing and a curse," Ásta continued, interrupting her musings.

"You had a love?" Neither Ásta nor Rúna had ever mentioned such a thing in all of the time that they'd spent together. What had happened? It pained her to think that they had kept this hidden from her. What other secrets did Ásta hide?

The comb paused mid-stroke. When Ásta spoke, her voice was heavy with sorrow. "I was married once, but he died."

"That is dreadful, Ásta. I had no idea." Heaviness filled her chest at the loss that undoubtedly still pained her friend greatly.

"It was long ago." Ásta paused, and Samara heard the telltale intake of a fortifying breath before she changed the subject. "I see how you look at Valen, and how he watches you too. He has feelings for you."

Samara stiffened at once, her body buzzing under the impact of Ásta's words. "He watches me?"

Ásta laughed heartily and the deep melancholy of earlier melted away. "He can scarcely tear his eyes away."

"Nothing can come of it. I must—" Samara pulled the braid over her shoulder and spun around to face her friend. How did one explain the expectations placed on royal daughters to a handmaiden?

"Nei," Ásta interrupted, and then reached out and gripped her shoulders in both hands firmly.

"What?"

Ásta's tone was adamant when she continued. "The goddess

Freya has brought you together for a reason, Samara. If you love him, then embrace it."

"But—" Ásta did not understand that it was her duty, as had long been her people's custom, that she wed a man of her father's choosing.

"Don't think, feel what your heart wants. Love can vanish in a heartbeat and all that you are left with are memories, little glowing embers to light the path though the darkness and pain that follow. Love him while you can."

"Love him..." Samara whispered, under her breath. Dare she, just this once, cast aside duty for love?

CHAPTER TWELVE

SAMARA

*S*amara woke to the dawn birdsong drifting through the open window on the chilly breeze. Her heart skipped a beat. Last eve, she'd decided to heed Ásta's advice. This would be her last chance to bed a man of her choosing before her father married her off. She may never feel like this for a man again. No way would she live the rest of her life filled with regret because she was afraid to take a chance.

She sat up and threw off the blanket. She had to act fast. With each day that passed, her time with Valen lessened. She pulled on a clean woollen overdress, combed her hair, and rushed outside. Tonight she would seduce him.

Her stomach fluttered with anticipation as she ducked beneath the branch of an apple tree, rushed across the grass, and into the great hall. She was later than usual to break her fast, but Valen may have waited to dine with her.

"Samara!"

Her father's deep guttural tone stopped her in her tracks— the Caliph had arrived. Her eyes instantly dropped to the floor in the deferential reflex ingrained from years in the Abbasid court. As she exhaled a heavy breath her shoulders slumped, all lightness and joy abandoning her as the heavy burden of duty returned.

"Are you well, daughter?"

Nei. She felt like saying it aloud. *Go away. I'm not ready to leave yet.* Instead, she straightened her shoulders and looked at the father she'd always adored.

His mouth was a grim line, his troubled eyes surrounded by deep wrinkles produced by age and harsh desert sun. He looked older and more weary than she remembered, and less intimidating. Not long ago she would have done anything for his favor, but no more.

"Samara?" When she didn't respond, her father rose from his seat at the table, his long white robes giving the impression he was floating as he signalled his Haras guards to remain in position against the wall and walked toward her.

He'd betrayed her. He'd let her believe that he would always keep her at his side because he trusted and valued her council. The moment that he'd said she needed to marry so she'd have a husband to protect her, her adoration had disappeared like the sun over the horizon never to rise again. He'd promised her freedom, only to snatch it away.

"Daughter?" He tilted his head as he approached her.

As she looked at the dark shadows beneath his eyes, her heart sank. Now that he was here, everything would change. She let him pull her into an embrace and glanced over his shoulder.

Valen sat at the table beside the seat her father had vacated, his expression devoid of emotion, the soft lips that had set her body alight pressed together in a harsh line.

Her chest tightened. His face confirmed what she already knew—her father's arrival had ended their agreement. She'd lost him.

Her father pulled back and looked at her, holding her shoulders in his hands. "Daughter, are you hurt?" he asked, in the familiar cadence of her native tongue so the Vikings could not understand.

She quelled the longing for his approval that threatened to creep back in and stiffened in his arms. "Father. I am well."

"These savages did not touch you?" His face was grim, as though he imagined her suffering through a terrifying ordeal.

She bristled at his unjust assumption, until she remembered that not long ago she would have thought the same and judged the Vikings unfairly.

"La." She shook her head. "All have treated me kindly."

He pinned her with a pensive stare. "Is this truth?"

She held his gaze and nodded firmly. "Yes. I promise, Father. I have been treated well."

The tension eased from his body as he released a relieved sigh. "I am glad to hear that, but I will feel better when you are back within the safety of the palace."

She pressed two fingers to her temple where her head ached. Her father loved her, but he demanded control of everybody around him and already she could feel the walls closing in around her. The daughter that her father knew would have forgotten the handsome Viking warrior and played the dutiful daughter, but she couldn't be that girl anymore.

Her father spun around as though his word was law and crossed the room to the seat he'd vacated.

She sighed, and then followed him, looking around the hall.

Her father, Valen, and his parents sat at the table with just a few handmaidens serving food, but the room was otherwise empty, empty and soulless without the raucous laughter and playful banter of the Viking clan.

She lowered herself into the chair beside her father. If she couldn't be who she was before, then who was she? She crossed her arms and leaned back in her chair, glaring at the angular lines of Valen's profile until he turned and looked at her.

He raised an eyebrow.

CHAPTER 12

Her blood boiled. How dare he act as if he had no idea why she was angry? He could keep their secret without pretending that she did not exist. He knew well that his aloof act would ignite her temper.

Valen's eyes flicked to her father the moment the Caliph shifted in his seat and turned to face him.

She held her tongue and watched, curious to see how he would handle this first meeting with her father.

"Jarl Eriksson. Samara assures me she is well, but where are my daughter's companions?"

Valen glanced at his parents. After a hardly noticeable head shake from his father, he replied without rectifying the Caliph's mistake in addressing him with the title he would not officially hold until later in the week. "Many of the women were too wounded to travel here immediately. I have had word from my men that they will arrive soon."

Samara nodded when Ásta looked at her questioningly and motioned at the empty cup on the table in front of her. Valen's words had ignited a spark of hope inside her. Her father would not leave until her companions arrived. There may be time yet for her and Valen to be together.

The Caliph nodded, though it was clear he was displeased with the delay this would cause to his schedule. "Then let us discuss trade."

Samara picked up the cup and sipped at the spiced mead the Vikings drank with the morning meal. Valen had never hidden his desire to negotiate a trade agreement with the Caliph. Even though she was angry with him, she was glad that he was getting the audience with the Caliph that he needed.

Valen inclined his head. "Today I would show you our hospitality. There is time enough for trade on the morrow."

Her fingers tightened on the cup as she stiffened. *La!* Nobody ever dismissed the Caliph.

His face remained calm, but she saw her father's hands

clench beneath the table. When her father rose from his seat, his Haras guards snapped to attention behind them. The Caliph inclined his head, his flawless manners that of a respectful guest.

"Until then, as you suggested, we will make camp in the meadow beyond the wall. Come, Samara."

Her jaw clenched. She debated ignoring his command but eventually rose from her seat and followed. Now was not the right time to voice her displeasure. She lifted her skirts as she walked across the rough stones that surrounded the central hearth, the hairs on the back of her neck standing on end. She could feel Valen watching her. Was his gaze lit with desire now that the danger of her father's watchful gaze was gone? A shiver crept up her spine as she paused and looked back over her shoulder.

He *was* watching her, but his gaze was vacant and dismissive, as though she was naught but a stranger.

Her stomach dropped. She'd never seen this side to him— here was the ruthless Viking that would rule the Eriksson clan. His cold gaze spoke volumes. Any affection he felt for her had died the moment the Caliph arrived. Hopelessness settled over her like a dark cloud and she turned to leave. Their agreement was over. Valen would never risk losing a powerful ally over a woman. She didn't want to let him go, but he felt nothing for her. She'd been a fool to think otherwise.

Valen shifted in his seat, the screech of his chair scraping on the stone floor making her pause and look closer.

He lounged comfortably in his chair, his expression distant, but his left eyebrow quivered slightly, just as it had when he'd attempted to trick her at Hnefatafl.

He was hiding the truth. Her heart beat faster. He didn't want to let her go either.

~

*V*alen kept his clenched fists hidden beneath the table as Samara walked towards the doorway. This felt like when he'd lost Kalda, but worse, much worse. This time Samara wasn't being stolen from him by death and violence, he was letting her go. He would know that she still lived and spent the rest of her days in the arms of another man. He flexed his aching hands.

Caliph Radi al-Abbasid had a commanding presence. He'd stomped into the longhouse in his white robes, flanked by his personal guard of hardened warriors, and pinned him with a stare that would have crushed a weaker man.

"Where is my daughter?" he'd demanded.

Within seconds of meeting the Caliph, Valen knew that the man would go to war for Samara. He would lay waste to Gottland unless he got his daughter back.

"Lulea, find Samara."

As the girl rushed from the room, the tension had left the Caliph's rigid shoulders. That momentary break in the man's regal armor had told him everything he needed to know about the man—he loved his daughter. It would hurt to watch Samara leave, but at least she was going with a man who would love and protect her. She belonged with her family, just as he belonged here with his.

Fortunately, the Caliph had arrived before they'd crossed a line that couldn't be undone. It had crushed him watching her joy-filled eyes widen at the sight of her father, and then dim as she realized what that meant.

When she'd leaned back at the table and stared at him with those amber eyes of hers, he'd forced himself to remain detached, knowing that it was for the best. There was no point delaying the inevitable, it would just hurt them both. Now, his chest was painfully tight as he watched her walk toward the door that would take her away from him forever.

She paused near the hearth, the top half of her body twisting as she looked back at him. Her eyes were sharp and assessing as she searched his face for any hint of the affection that had grown between them, for a sign that he still cared for her.

He kept his expression blank. They'd both agreed that this would stop when her father arrived. She might have changed her mind, but he must honor his deal with her and put a stop to the dangerous game they'd been playing.

Hurt flared in her eyes.

He forced himself not to react. He wanted to leap across the table, take her in his arms, and kiss away the hurt he had caused. She was in his blood now, a part of him, but he knew that the longer this thing between them continued, the more it would hurt her when it ended. And it would end, it had to end.

The air thickened, awareness pulsing between them as she tilted her head and narrowed her eyes. Then her lips curved upward in a knowing smile and she spun around and disappeared outside.

His plate jumped as he smacked his hand on the wooden tabletop. Blasted woman was entirely too smart—she'd seen straight through him.

CHAPTER THIRTEEN

SAMARA

*S*amara weaved through the tables in the great hall and slowly edged her way across the crowded room. The deft fingers of the Caliph's master musician strummed and plucked at the strings of the oud in accompaniment to the evening's entertainment.

She watched her father sway back and forth to the music in his chair at the head table. He was distracted. His attention, along with every warrior in the room, was on his favorite belly dancer, Rahinda, as she twirled and swayed her hips in a seductive dance.

Samara slipped into the shadows and skirted the edge of the room. Now was the time to disappear. The wild revelry would continue all night, and anybody who noticed her absence would think she had retired early.

"Valen?" She placed a hand on his back, ensuring she remained hidden behind a large wooden pillar. For hours, she'd watched him move around the room, pausing to talk and toast with his guests, but once they were finally sated he'd retreated to a corner to watch over the festivities.

His back stiffened beneath her hand, and then he slowly turned to face her.

"I must talk to you." She looked up at him, resisting the urge to remove the orange and yellow veil that hid all but her eyes from him. Before her time here, she'd thought nothing of putting on the traditional veil and gown of her people, but now it made her feel like she was suffocating. She missed the flare of desire that lit his blue eyes when he looked upon her face.

"It is unwise, Samara." His head turned, his gaze drifting to where her father grinned at a woman perched on his lap, feeding him a fig.

"He'll not notice," she whispered. "I cannot leave with this distance between us. Please come meet me away from here."

He ran a hand through his hair. "Where?"

"At the north gate," she said, and then walked away before he could argue, her stomach fluttering as she made her way toward the door. She'd done it. There was no turning back now. It was time to take what she wanted. She wanted Valen to claim her body, she wanted him to show her what it was like to be with a man, and she was going to make that happen...tonight.

"I don't have long. What do you want to talk about?" Valen said when he met her beneath the stone arch of the north gate a short while later.

She grabbed his hand and tugged him along behind her. Now that he was here, she would not give him the chance to change his mind.

"Sama—"

"Shhh," she hushed him. She skirted the shadows of the encampment in the meadow beyond the north gate. Then tiptoed quietly, barely daring to breathe as they passed near the fire where the Haras guards warmed themselves between rotations.

"Samara," Valen hissed. "I can't be here."

She squeezed his hand until her fingers ached, praying he got the message to be quiet. He was going to get them both killed if they were caught. She continued moving through the sea of tents. Nothing would halt her now, not when she was so close.

He tugged his hand from hers. "Samara. Where are we going?"

"Shh." She grabbed a lit lantern from where it hung outside a tent waiting for the occupants to return, and led him to her private tent. She lifted the flap to make an opening.

"Hurry, get in."

He shook his head. "Nei."

Her temper flared. Once they were inside her tent, they'd be safe—nobody would dare enter her private quarters uninvited. She couldn't let his stubborn need to do the right thing ruin everything. She'd learned well from him—she wouldn't play fair tonight.

"It will be worse if they see you."

He backed away. He was going to run.

She risked a glance around the corner of the tent—they were still alone, but for how long? "If we go inside we can talk freely. The guards only roam the camp boundary, and nobody else will return until near dawn."

"But..."

She huffed. She could not let him get them caught. She grabbed his hand again, bent at the waist, and pulled him through the narrow opening and into her tent.

"Samara," he scolded her, and pulled his hand from hers.

She secured the door from the inside, and then ignored him as she stood on tiptoes to hang the lantern from the hook hanging near the doorway.

When she turned to face him, he was touching the fabric that lined the inside of her tent, admiring the elaborate orange and gold pattern that shimmered in the soft light.

Her heart jumped at the sight of him, a tall masculine warrior curiously inspecting the delicately woven fabric.

"It seems your father withheld some of his finest treasures from me in today's negotiations," he said gruffly.

She walked to the large carpet covered in large sheepskin rugs and many large silk cushions. "It was made by the women of a Bedouin tribe that roam the desert. I will see that some are included with the other wares."

He remained still, his eyes following her every move.

"Come sit." She lowered herself onto a cushion with her knees to the side and tucked up behind her, and then patted the cushion beside her.

"Why are we here, Samara?" His brow furrowed as he stared at the sheer white curtains that fell from the ceiling, hiding all but a glimpse of the red mosaic bedcover and matching pillows atop her bed.

Her stomach fluttered. She raised an eyebrow at him questioningly. He'd never admit it, but she knew he'd pictured them on the bed together.

"We should not be alone—this is not what we agreed. I thought you wanted to say farewell. I'd not have agreed if I'd known you would bring me here."

"We are here now. Come and sit, so we may talk."

His eyes flicked to the tent opening before he began to move toward her.

She shivered, admiring the muscles of his powerful thighs and the bulge that lay between them as he walked toward her. His body was as hard as carved stone, and much finer even than the much-lauded statues of the god Óðinn that the Vikings worshipped.

Valen lowered himself beside her, his legs outstretched and crossed at the ankles.

"I knew that you would insist on honoring our agreement..." Her heart raced. She wanted Valen to accept what she was about to offer, more than anything she'd ever desired. She shuffled closer to him, until their thighs touched, and then reached out to touch his hair. "...But I am no longer agreeable to the terms."

"What are you saying?" His voice was the rough and raspy growl of a man fighting for control.

She swept her fingers down along his jawline and the soft hair of his beard. "I don't want to stop spending time with you."

His hands clenched into fists and he shook his head. "We cannot. It is too dangerous."

"Valen..." she whispered, letting her yearning hang on that one desperate plea. She inhaled a shaky breath, threw aside caution, and bared herself to him. "You promised me nothing is forbidden. I cannot live my life without ever bedding a man of my choosing."

He jerked back at her words.

She needed to show him that she meant what she said. She reached up and unfastened the gold-and-gem-encrusted clasp that held her veil in place, and then slowly unwrapped the shimmering scarf and let it slide through her fingers and fall to the carpet.

His eyes widened. "What are you doing?"

Good. She had him off balance. Now she had to keep him that way. She reached out and stroked his thigh, feeling the hard muscle tense beneath the fabric. Satisfaction filled her when he shuddered and then hastily brushed her hand away. He wanted her.

"Nei, we cannot. Your father..."

"Shh." Samara pressed a finger to his lips. "All we will ever have are these moments." This was her life and her body, and she wanted her first lover to be him. In her heart, she knew that he would be the gentle and kind lover that she needed. Determined not to let him push her away out of some misplaced sense of honor, she rose up onto her knees, gathered her skirts and straddled his thighs.

A deep growl rumbled from his chest as she lowered herself down over the hard evidence of his desire.

"Nei." His hands wrapped around her waist. He was going to push her off.

She placed her hands on his shoulders and looked down into his angst-ridden eyes. She couldn't bear to hear him refuse her. She needed this, needed him.

"I want you," she whispered.

He swallowed hard and blinked, his hands tightening as he hesitated. He was conflicted and likely fighting his own sense of honor and duty, but she could convince him.

"Do not deny me, Valen. I need you, all of you."

She rocked forward, gasping at the wave of pleasure that ignited where her flesh pressed against his thickness. Her blood heated and rushed through her veins like a firestorm, until an uncontrollable shudder wracked her body.

"I know you want me too."

CHAPTER FOURTEEN

VALEN

*A*s Samara's eyes drifted closed and she rocked backward along his hard length, Valen felt the last of his tenuous resolve shatter. Samara wanted him, and he couldn't deny himself any longer. He had to have her, no matter the consequences.

"Já. I am yours." He grasped her slender hips and pulled her forward.

"Oh…"

He gave a knowing grin at her husky moan. He hungered to lick the sweet taste of her juices from his lips, and feel the silky slide of her skin beneath him. He'd be the first to show her the joys of lovemaking. He would make it good. He could give her that.

He tugged at the masses of yellow and orange patterned fabric wrapped around her.

"Let me." She brushed him away, her hands working quickly to remove the garment and toss it aside, leaving her entirely bared to him.

His cock hardened even more. Óðinn take him now—she was naked and he could see the glistening evidence of her desire. He ran his hands along the smooth expanse of her tanned legs, over the enticing curves of her hip, and up to cup her full breasts. She was breathtaking, the kind of beauty that brought men to their knees. He brushed his thumbs across the tips of her dark nipples and watched them furl into tight buds.

"Valen..."

He fought back the victorious cry that threatened to overcome him at the desperate breathy sound of his name falling from her lips, then cupped the back of her head and lowered his lips to hover over hers.

"I know what you need, Princess," he growled. Heat flooded his body as he claimed her mouth, gently coaxing it open with unhurried strokes of his tongue.

Unwilling to accept his slow pace, she bit down on his bottom lip, making his heart race. She wanted him with a passion that matched his own. She covered his mouth with hers and her tongue darted out in commanding strokes as she devoured him.

He groaned and let her take what she needed, though his heart beat so fast that he thought it would explode if she took much more. Finally, when he felt his body nearing release, he pulled away.

"Not so fast."

She squirmed in his lap in protest, the press of her soft folds against the outline of his hard cock in his breeches wrenching another growl from his chest. By the gods, he had to slow this down, or the woman would be his undoing. He flipped them over, laying her back on the silk cushions and settling between her legs.

"Don't stop," she begged, looking up at him.

"I won't," he promised. He couldn't have stopped even if he'd wanted to—rational thought had deserted him long ago. He pulled off his shirt, desperate to feel the heat of her skin against his chest. He inhaled the exotic musky perfume in the curve of her neck and laid a path of soft kisses downward.

She clutched his head in her hands, her fingers tangling in his hair to keep him in place as he swirled his tongue around one puckered nipple and his fingers plucked at the furled bud of the other.

"Já. That feels amazing."

He was just getting started. He knew what she needed. He licked his lips and took her nipple into his mouth, sucking in the primal rhythm he knew would make her ache.

She writhed beneath him as she surrendered to the pleasure. Slowly her body tensed, and then her breath quickened, her chest rising rapidly as she neared the edge.

He released her breast and rose above her on his forearms. She looked like a bronzed goddess, with one hand thrown up over her head and her skin flushed from the rough touch of his beard. A smile tugged at the corners of his mouth. He'd done that to her. He'd made her limp with desire.

Her dark eyelashes fluttered and her eyes slowly opened.

The noise of his heart beating in his ears was deafening as he saw his own fervent need reflected back at him. He moved down her body and settled on the rug between her legs.

"What are you...?"

He studied her glistening sex as he slid his hands across her waist to hold her still. He could smell the sweetness of her desire.

"I must taste you."

"What?" Her knees came up as she moved to shield herself from him and shook her head.

"Trust me? I'll make you feel good."

"I trust you." She watched him warily, but let him guide her legs back down.

Gently, he slid his hands up and brushed his thumbs over her nipples until her eyelids fluttered closed. She gasped as he pressed his mouth to her sex, sliding his tongue along her folds and delving inside in search of her honey. She tasted sweet and creamy—he couldn't get enough.

"Oh." She threw her head back when his tongue caressed her swollen nub, and then cried out again when he suckled slowly with long hard strokes.

His chest swelled with pride as she began to toss back and forth, her dark hair falling in gentle waves across her breasts. He longed to release his hard cock from his breeches, but he ignored his own needs and held her firmly in place. He wouldn't let her down now, not when she was so close. He pressed his tongue against her and flicked.

She tensed, her mouth falling open in a silent cry as she shuddered. Never had a woman looked as beautiful as her in that the moment.

Something shifted near his heart as he watched her soar. This woman had found a way into the secret place he'd sworn he'd never open again. When a satisfied smile settled on her face, he lay down beside her and pulled a blanket over them both. He ran his fingers up and down her arm.

She raised her hands above her head and stretched before rolling on her side and throwing a leg across his waist.

"That was…"

"Já." He wrapped an arm around her, ignoring the brush of her bare breasts against his chest, and grinned at her loss for words.

"But you didn't… We didn't finish."

He pressed a finger to her lips and shook his head. This was about her pleasure, it always had been.

Her eyes twinkled as she slid her tongue along his finger, and then sucked it into her warm mouth down to the knuckle.

Óðinn! The hair on the back of his neck stood on end at the wanton look in her eyes as she pressed her tongue against it and then released him. How did the woman know about taking a man in her mouth? What in Hel had Rúna and Ásta been teaching her?

"I want to, Valen. I don't want to wonder what could have been. I want *everything* with you." Her fingers drifted down over the ridges of his muscular stomach.

His skin heated beneath her touch. The thought of claiming her was so dangerous, so tempting, that he could hear his own heart pounding in his ears.

"Everything?"

She nodded slowly, and then her hand skimmed the waistband of his pants and dropped to unbutton his breeches. "Everything..."

He groaned and crushed his mouth on hers. He'd never wanted a woman as much as he wanted her. Their mouths moved in a frantic dance as she pushed his breeches down and he kicked them off.

Her hands tugged at his shoulders until he rolled atop her, his throbbing cock cradled in her slick heat.

Mother of Óðinn. What was he doing? He cupped her face in his hands and gently brushed his thumbs across her cheeks. The urge to join with her was impossible to resist. He pulled back and raised himself above her, his arms shaking as the head of his staff aligned with the place he was desperate to invade.

"Oh." The soft sigh fell from her lips.

He swallowed hard and looked down at her. There was no turning back after they did this. Now that they were here, she deserved the chance to change her mind. He raised an eyebrow.

Her eyes widened briefly at his unasked question. She looked down to where their bodies met, then back up at him with unrestrained desire. Her breasts jiggled as she curled her fingers around his wrists.

"Everything," she whispered.

"Já, Princess. I will give you everything." He slowly rocked forward until he slid into her warm heat. She was everything he had imagined, Valhalla on earth—warm, tight, and wet. When she sucked in a shaky breath as he met the barrier of her innocence, he lowered to his forearms and kissed her deep and demanding, until she relaxed and cautiously rocked her hips. He rose above her once more. He was loath to hurt her, but she was ready. He grit his teeth and plunged deep.

Her eyes widened and she stiffened, crying out as her body clamped down on him. Her nails dug into the tender flesh of his wrists and the metallic tang of blood filled the air.

"The worst is over. Breathe, just breathe." He ignored the pain, knowing that hers was much worse, and held himself frozen above her.

She looked up at him through teary eyes and sucked in shaky breaths.

He wouldn't move, even if it killed him. He'd do nothing more to hurt her. As her breathing slowed and the tension eased from her body, he lowered himself to rest on his forearms and trailed wet kisses down her neck. "You undo me."

She shivered and wrapped her arms around his neck.

Good. She was ready to move beyond the pain. "You are the sweetest treat," he whispered, then scraped his teeth across the tender flesh of her earlobe and sucked it into his mouth.

She moaned and arched her back, her hard nipples brushing against his chest as she rocked her hips against him.

"Já." He lost himself in her, rocking back, and then thrusting forward as he felt the bond between them growing as though infused with the magic of the gods as together they found a rhythm.

Her hips rose to meet his, her hands sliding down to his backside and then pulling him into her faster.

If she didn't stop, he would be spent. He couldn't let that happen, not when it would leave her wanting. He slid his hands beneath her and rolled onto his back.

She froze above him, the flickering light of the lantern

casting shimmering light across her skin and the rich tones of the gold and orange drapery hanging from the center of the tent roof.

The gods had opened the gates to Valhalla to give him a taste of paradise. She'd wanted this night together, so it felt right that she would be the one to take them both to release.

"Like this." He put his hands on her hips and rocked her along his length.

Her eyes widened in surprise.

By the gods, he was so close already. "Now sit up."

She placed her hands in the center of his chest and pushed herself upright. Her long hair fell down around her until the tips slid across his thighs like silky fingers and stole the air from his lungs.

"Take what you want." He grasped her firm ass and guided her motions, showing her how to rise up and thrust herself back down on him.

Her lips parted, and a soft moan slipped free as her eyes drifted closed and she began to bounce with slow deliberate strokes.

He clenched his teeth and reached up to cup her breasts, plucking at her nipples as he fought back his own release. Then he slid his hand down her stomach and through the soft hair that hid her swollen nub, and feasted on her nipples as he worked her furiously. The more he tasted, the more he craved her. He thrust upward, pumping his hips hard and fast. He couldn't stop now—he was past the point of no return.

Then she collapsed forward, her nails digging into his chest as she quickened her pace. She was close.

"Já," he groaned, and bit down on her nipple, giving her just enough pain to send her catapulting into bliss.

She arched her back and cried out as she began to quiver around him.

He lost all reason as her slick heat squeezed his cock. He

thrust once, twice more, and joined her, muffling his throaty roar against her neck as he exploded inside her.

A few minutes later, she pulled the blanket up over them and cuddled into his side with her head on his chest. "Is it always like that?"

What should he tell her? Their lovemaking, and he had no doubt that's what it was, had shaken him to his core. He shook his head.

"Nei. That was everything...and more." He cradled her in his arms and cupped the smooth globes of her ass.

"Much more," she whispered in agreement.

He watched as her eyes drifted closed and she fell asleep. Damn the gods and their spiteful games—now that he knew she was perfect for him it would destroy him to watch her leave.

CHAPTER FIFTEEN

SAMARA

*S*amara held the quill over the parchment, eager to
record the final few trades and escape to back to her
tent. She fought the urge to rub her hand over her face. Would
this meeting ever end? For hours, Valen had sampled the
various spices and foods available on the Silk Road as she'd
mediated the negotiations and recorded the details of their
trades on the parchment resting on the small wooden table
across her knees.

The Caliph leaned back in his chair. "It is a fair price for a
rare spice."

You can do this, just a little longer. She sighed inwardly. It was
exhausting maintaining the peace between her father and Valen
whilst hiding her attraction to the Viking Jarl. She could not
fail. She didn't want to think of the consequences of her father
discovering their illicit affair. She lowered her lashes to hide her
uneasiness—nothing could jeopardize the trade deal for Valen.

"You ask for too much gold for such a small jar," Valen
insisted, holding the Caliph's penetrating gaze.

The Caliph sipped his wine, his long fingers tapping on the
side of the cup in a movement that exuded power and elegance.

It was a carefully crafted tactic intended to intimidate his oppo-
nent. Unfortunately for him, it was having little effect on Valen.

Watching them quibble over a tiny jar of saffron reminded
her of two strutting roosters fighting for dominance, and her
patience was long gone.

"Must you argue over every item?" she said, waving her hand
at the table still covered in items they had yet to discuss. "We
will be here all day."

Valen sat back and crossed his arms over his chest, his blue
eyes boring into hers.

She looked away, attempting to douse the heat that pooled
between her legs. How was she supposed to pretend there was
nothing between them when he looked at her like that?

Don't look. As long as she did not look at him, she could hide
how she felt. If their secret was safe, then there was no reason
not to continue their affair until she left.

Do. Not. Look. She could do that.

She turned to her father. "There must be compromise on
both sides," she said, raising an eyebrow at him. He was over-
charging for the saffron and could easily drop the price and still
make well above market value for the item.

"What has come over you, Daughter?" he replied, with a
flicker of warning in his dark eyes.

"I merely seek a fair resolution for all."

"You would lessen our profits and take food from the
mouths of your own people, just because of the hospitality you
received here?" Though her father left the rest of his thoughts
unspoken, she could tell that he was questioning if her loyalties
had shifted. His expression was cold as he picked up the jar and
removed the lid.

Her eyes drifted closed as the earthy aroma of the spice
tickled her nostrils, a sudden wave of nostalgia crashing over
her—saffron rice, watching the shifting desert sands from her
balcony, and the laughter of her people washing in the Tigris.

"I will trade for the spices and other stores..." Valen said.

She blinked and opened her eyes. The soft rumble of his voice brought memories of last eve flooding back—his hands on her body, the hard planes of his golden chest hovering above her. Her heart raced as she recalled the caress of his beard across her skin that had left her feeling utterly lost, yet with no desire whatsoever to be found. If his gentle lovemaking had been a ploy to make her want him even more, she did.

Her father inclined his head. "A wise choice—"

Valen held up his hand to interrupt and stroked his beard as though deep in thought.

The Caliph's jaw tensed, and then a gleeful shine lit his eyes as Valen dragged out the extended pause until it bordered on rude. He was enjoying this battle of the wits with the Viking Jarl. Valen may not be as schooled at negotiation, but he had a natural instinct for the thrust and parry of the game and the Caliph's respect for him had grown as the morning progressed.

"...But I will only pay half. And I will also take the silks and the beads," Valen finally finished. His gaze never strayed from the Caliph or the goods on the table between them as he shifted in his seat and casually crossed his outstretched legs at the ankle.

She looked down at the parchment to hide her smile. Valen was no fool. Whenever the Caliph became distracted, Valen wielded these surprise tactics with timely precision to spark his interest and keep him at the table.

The Caliph held Valen's gaze. "Half for the saffron and you will take *all* of the silks. They are of the finest quality. I will gift thirty just like these to Samara's future husband. They will make a fine gift for your woman."

Samara stiffened at her father's exaggeration—they were far from the finest silks that were traded on the Silk Road. And curse him for reminding her of her impending marriage. She knew that he thought he was doing what was best for her by finding her a husband, but his lack of consideration for her opinion on the matter was infuriating. She was a grown woman, not a child. Valen at least respected her enough to allow her to make her own decisions.

"Indeed they would make a fine gift," Valen replied.

Her eyes flicked between the two of them, the shrewd reserved leader and the fierce Viking warrior, forthright and bound by honor, they couldn't be more different. What should she do? She wanted to warn Valen that it was not a fair trade, but doing so would be betraying her people. *Her* people... She was an Abbasid princess—they deserved her loyalty. Her head began to ache with the pressure of being caught between two different worlds.

Valen raised his cup to his mouth as his eyes met hers over the rim. "I am yet to wed, but they are for someone special."

Sparks flew between them. The hair on the nape of her neck stood on end. He was talking about her. She glanced at her father, hoping that he had not noticed.

His dark eyes narrowed as his gaze flicked between her and Valen suspiciously.

Her stomach dropped, all remnants of her lingering desire vanishing as a deathly chill swept through the tent. She'd been a fool to think that she could continue to walk in two worlds without consequence. It would tear her in two if she continued, and even worse, destroy both of their worlds if her father found out. She had to stop this dangerous affair, now.

Valen drained his cup and set it on the table.

She motioned for it to be refilled, and then looked down at her quill, squeezing it between her fingertips until they ached. As much as it would hurt, she knew what she needed to do. She would play the cold distant Princess until Valen understood it was over between them.

"I am sure your wife, when you choose one, will love them," she said dismissively.

When she looked up, his heated stare and the flare of his nostrils spoke volumes. She glanced over at her father, and then back at him. Her meaning clear, this cannot be, not here, not now, never again.

"That she will," he said, then turned to her father and continued as though her rebuff was of no consequence to him. "I will have all the silks."

The breath rushed from her lungs as she looked down and added the silks to the tally on the parchment. What a fool she had been to forget that Valen too would soon wed another. Inside she was drowning, sinking into the abyss as she broke under the loss of everything she'd ever wanted—Valen, friends, freedom, love.

Love...

The soft whisper in her mind was undeniable—she loved Valen. Over these last weeks, she had fallen in love with the formidable Viking Jarl, and now she must let him go. She swallowed her despair and fought to maintain her mask of bland indifference.

"Caliph, I will have my men deliver the wares to your camp."

"Good. Good." Her father waved his hand absently.

"And you have my word that I will send you those warriors willing to fight for you next summer," Valen continued.

"How do we know you will follow through?" Her voice shook as she asked the question her father would expect, barely keeping control of the grief clawing at her insides. Why did making the right decision feel so wrong?

Valen leaned back and raised an eyebrow at her. "I always keep my promises, Princess."

She shivered as the deep rumble of his voice washed over her. *What was he saying?*

"Caliph, I know you are a man of your word. I am sure we can have open, honest negotiations. The men will require gold for their services, but they will fight well for you."

A flush of heat warmed her cheeks as the hidden meaning in Valen's words hit her—of the two of them, it was she who had lied about her identity. She welcomed the bite of her fingernails digging into her palms. The man needed reminding that he wasn't a pillar of honesty either.

"Shall I have your goods delivered to the north tower?" she asked, her voice thick with saccharine sweetness. A surge of triumph filled her when his jaw tensed at the mention of where he had first tasted her.

Before he could respond, Fareed, head of the Haras guard, stepped inside and bowed. "Pardon the interruption. I must speak with you, Caliph."

Her father rose to his feet. "One moment please, Jarl. I shall return," he said, and then crossed to the far side of the tent conversing in hushed whispers with his most trusted man.

"So, the delivery?" she prompted. It would be faster to finish the last trades without her father here to argue every detail, and she wanted this over. She could not continue to look at him much longer without falling apart.

Valen nodded at her, his lips curving up slightly in the corners. "Já. Deliver them to the tower. Have you tasted peaches, Princess?" He plucked one from the basket he'd brought along. "They are the first of the season. Picked fresh by Inga this morning."

"Peaches?" She frowned at the abrupt change of topic and looked down at her notes. What was he doing? She had recorded the peaches trade hours ago.

"You must try one." He cut the fruit into pieces with his dagger, and placed it on the plate in front of her.

She set down the quill and eyed him warily. What game was he playing?

"Try it," he urged.

She took a piece and cautiously bit down. The rush of soft

delicate sweetness filled her mouth and almost made her groan aloud.

Delicious. "I've never tasted anything so sweet."

When he shifted in his seat, her eyes flicked down to the prominent bulge of his groin. She looked away so he couldn't see her blushing cheeks.

"I have, Princess. I've tasted the sweetest forbidden fruit."

Her eyes snapped back to his, following the slide of his tongue across his lips, the flush of her skin deepening further. Her heart raced as her body warmed. She picked up the quill, resisting the urge to crush it between her fingers. The temptation he presented seriously tested her newly-formed resolve. She'd been very clear that this could not go on and she knew he'd understood.

"Do not do this," she demanded, her tone icy. He was chasing her because she had denied him, but she would not be his plaything. No matter how thrilling it was to be chased by the Viking, he would not conquer her.

"Would you rather negotiate Viking steel?" He lounged back casually in the chair, ensuring his hips thrust up to display the hard length of his member pressing against the front of his pants.

She stilled at the sight, her nipples hardening against the fabric covering her bust. *Do. Not. Look.* She could not react. He would sense even the slightest weakness and use it to get her to concede, to continue the affair. She schooled her features and twirled the quill absently.

"Mayhap..." she said, feigning indifference.

When he grinned knowingly, she knew she had failed. He knew he was affecting her and now he would press his advantage.

"Do you want Viking steel, Princess?"

Her breath hitched at the double entendre, but she refused to yield. The affair must stop, for both their sakes. Instead, she raised an eyebrow and pinned him with the chilly unimpressed stare she'd perfected at court. If he continued with these underhanded ploys, he would soon find himself severely outmatched.

"The price is too high." She opened her mouth and slid another slice of peach inside, deliberately chewing slowly and then licking the juices from her lips.

He swallowed hard, his eyes following her every move. "Some things are priceless," he croaked, and then hastily rose to his feet as the Caliph approached.

"Forgive me, Jarl. A matter requires my immediate attention. I must leave it to Samara to finish the negotiations."

Valen inclined his head. "I too must return to my duties, however I can meet with Samara later this eve to conclude our business. My apologies, but as I am sure you understand, the demands of being Jarl are many."

Blasted man! She knew what he was doing. That was no invitation to negotiate, it was a ruse to get her alone again.

"Indeed they are," her father replied as he shook Valen's hand. When he turned to face her, her stomach dropped at the disappointment and doubt she saw in his eyes.

"Do what is best for our people, Daughter. Remember Karim should you falter."

To Valen it meant naught, but the mention of the man that had betrayed her to Leif made her gut churn. The warning was plain—if she were a traitor she would suffer the same fate as Karim and be forever banished from court and ostracized.

Samara nodded and watched her father leave with Fareed. Her chest ached at the thought of never seeing her lands or people again. She missed the cheeky smiles of the children peeking out from behind their mother's skirts in the bazaar, the soft breeze on her skin as she sat under the night sky, and the heartfelt songs of the gypsy musicians, the kawlīyya. Home. She missed home. The threat of losing everything she loved was more than she could bear. She could not betray her people, she would not.

She rose to her feet. "I cannot come to your room," she told Valen, her tone colder than a winter storm. "This is over. Soon I will return home and marry. We have been playing a dangerous game. It has to stop. Every sun must set."

"The peaches are a gift," he replied, and then leaned in close.

The heat of his breath on her ear made heat pool between her legs. Curse him for being harder to resist than cardamom coffee on a cold morning.

"I will wait for you this eve. I hope you will come." The ravenous glint in his eyes as he pulled back spoke volumes—he was determined to get her back into his furs.

She backed away from him, shaking her head. "I cannot," she whispered, and then swallowed the sob in her throat when strode away.

CHAPTER SIXTEEN

VALEN

*V*alen paced back and forth in front of the fire, looking at the door. He'd sent his warriors out on patrols, claiming the additional guests warranted heightened watch, and then he'd walked along the wall, debating his good judgement. Would Samara come?

She had told him it was over, but he still hoped she would change her mind. He didn't know what had happened at the meeting with the Caliph that had made her pull away. Mayhap it was something he had said, or she thought being together was too perilous? Whatever it was, she had decided there would be nothing more between them. He stopped in the center of the room and ran his hands through his hair. She wasn't coming. He couldn't blame her, but it still hurt, more than he cared to admit.

A heartbeat later, the heavy oak door creaked and groaned open, letting in a cool draft.

"Valen?" Samara stepped inside, her small frame covered by the dark woollen cloak that fell to her feet.

He breathed deeply. She was here, probably wondering if it was a mistake to risk everything to be alone together, but she was here.

She closed the door, pushed back the hood that hid her face, and hesitated.

"I am glad you came." He crossed to where she stood and slid the metal bar into place across the door. None could bother them now. Wise or not, he'd made his decision that night in the tent with her and there was no turning back.

Her eyes darted nervously around his home.

"We are alone." He took her hand gently and linked his fingers though hers, the skin on skin contact creating a delicious shiver that made the hair on his neck stand on end.

The tension eased from her shoulders at his words. "I should not have come."

"Why did you?" Had she come for trade or because she wanted to see him? It felt like his heart stopped beating as he awaited her response.

"I could not stay away."

A swift and violent surge of triumph had him leading her hastily to the far end of the room before she could change her mind. His blood heated as he held back the drapery that provided privacy so she could enter his bedchamber.

She paused and looked up at him tenderly before stepping inside, her fingers brushing along the palm of his hand as though she couldn't bear to let go.

Loosening his grip on the fabric, he let it fall, shutting out the rest of the world. He watched her scan his bedchamber, taking in the glowing embers of the fire, two comfortable chairs near the hearth, and his bed covered in a pile of furs. When her eyes returned to his, they were lit with a fiery passion that matched his own.

"Let me take your cloak." In three strides, he was at her side and eased it from her shoulders. He swallowed hard as she walked away, her blue dress revealing womanly curves every bit as tantalising as her shimmering bronzed skin.

"By the gods, I need you." He had to have her, feel her in his arms again, and worship her. He tossed her cloak over a chair and moved toward her.

She backed away, the soft glow of the fire in her eyes reminding him of molten gold. "I want you too."

Before he even realized what he was doing, he'd pulled his shirt over his head, tossed it aside, and closed the distance between them. He reached for her, placing his hand beside her head as she bumped into the wall. His gaze fell to where her teeth bit into her bottom lip, and his chest vibrated as he held back his wild growl of approval. She liked him chasing her, this rougher more demanding side of him.

"I want to claim you, hard. But I'll not do that to you, not yet, not unless you ask."

Her eyes widened and a rush of pink stained her cheeks. "Já," she whispered.

"Princess..." He bent at the knees, wrapped an arm around her thighs, and lifted her. He was taking her to bed, now.

Her hands rested on his shoulders to steady herself. "What are you doing? Put me down."

"Very well." He loosened his grip, allowing her to slide slowly downward, his skin ablaze as her breasts brushed down over his bared chest.

"Not fair, Valen," she said, as her feet settled on the floor. Her hands rested softly on his chest, a cooling touch on the heated flesh beneath them.

"I don't follow rules." He grinned at her shamelessly. He'd felt the hardened peaks of her nipples through her dress, and her gasp when she'd felt the hard length of his cock pressed into her stomach. She wanted him too.

Her dark lashes lowered and her gaze fell to his lips. "I do like no rules."

Freya, have mercy. He needed to see her, feel her, *now.* In moments, he had her dress up over her head and tossed aside. He released a throaty groan, his cock hardening instantly.

"By the gods, woman. Where is your shift? You are naked."

She smiled demurely and ran her hands up his chest, hiding her breasts from his view. "You're not the only one with tricks."

"I shall show you tricks." He hoisted her up again, his hands cupping the firm globes of her ass as he crossed the room and lowered her into his bed.

"Promise?"

Had he died and gone to Valhalla? He'd known she was feisty, but he'd never thought she'd tease him like this in the bedchamber. She was so much more than he deserved, so damned perfect for him.

She stretched out across his bed like a lazy cat in the sunshine with her waves of dark hair fanned out behind her. Her eyes filled with lust as she watched him undress, her fingers trailing across the soft furs that caressed her bare flesh.

"See something you want?" he teased. He put his hands on his hips and stood proud for her inspection, relishing the heat in her gaze as she took in the sight of him.

She bit her lip. "Já, but I shouldn't."

"Nothing is forbidden between us, Princess." He slowly lowered himself between her legs, inhaling sharply as his hard cock pressed against her soft flesh. Then her arms wrapped around his neck and he was lost, lost to the press of her mouth on his, to the sensual dance of her tongue and the heated press of her beneath him. He deepened the kiss, unleashing all of his pent up need, and then dipped lower to suckle on her tender breasts. Thank Óðinn that this time he didn't need to go slow, that this time he could show her how a Viking satisfied his woman.

"Hurry." She writhed beneath him, the soft folds of her sex rubbing against his throbbing staff sending lightning bolts of pleasure through his body.

He slid his hand between her legs to prepare her. "Do you like this?"

"Já." Her eyes drifted closed as he pleasured her. Before long, her hands gripped his shoulders and urged him upward. "Now, Valen. I need you."

Unable to deny her desperate plea, he held himself above her, his eyes closing as his thick rod aligned with her sheath. He paused, rocking slightly back and forth to savor the sensation of her wetness and warmth along his length before he gave her what she wanted.

Her fingers dug into his chest. "Will it hurt?"

He looked down at her and shook his head, cursing himself. He should have known she would be afraid of the pain after last time. Her isolation and the secrecy of their affair meant she could not talk to her mother or a married relative to alleviate her fears.

"Not this time," he assured her.

Slowly, her hand curled up behind his neck to toy with his hair. "I trust you."

"Samara..." Her name fell from his lips as a reverent whisper. She trusted him with her body, and deep down he knew she was trusting him with her heart too. In that moment he resolved not to hold anything back from her, no matter how painful it would be when she left. He let down the barriers to his wounded heart, determined that his time he would make love to her with all his being, so that she would know what it felt like when two became one in bed.

Her hand stilled and she looked at him curiously. "What is it?"

"I trust you too."

Her eyes widened in surprise.

"Everything this time, Princess. All of me."

Tears filled her eyes as the weight of his words registered. "Everything..." she whispered.

"Já. Everything." Time slowed as he held her heated gaze and slid slowly into her wet heat, the two of them caught on the rising tide of honesty and raw emotion that flowed between them. He thrust slowly until she was breathless with pleasure, and then lowered himself to whisper in her ear.

"Slow is good ..." He rocked back, and then thrust hard. "But hard and fast is better."

"Oh!" she gasped as their hips met with a jolt, and then wrapped her legs around his waist.

"Let go." He slid his hands beneath her back and gripped her shoulders, loving the softness of her breasts sliding across his chest as he moved within her. He rested his head in the crook on her neck, breathed in the intoxicating scent of wild-flower soap on her skin, and showed her how a man loved a woman.

"Valen. Oh!" She matched his rhythm, her nails digging into his ass as she pulled him into her harder and faster than he dared. She was nearing the edge.

His heart raced as he lost all restraint, thrusting with increasing abandon until he reached a furious pounding that bordered in-between pleasure and pain. He could tell from her breathy moans that she was there with him, teetering on the edge of release.

"Let go," he urged, and then teased her nipple with his tongue and suckled on it hard.

She came apart in his arms, her back arching off the bed and her mouth falling open as she began to quiver around him.

He held her tight, one hand behind her back, the other between her breasts, and looked down at her as he thrust in to the hilt.

She was breathtaking—bronzed silky skin, mouth open in euphoric repose, full breasts thrust upward, and her face lit with utter abandon as she soared.

"Já!" He roared in blissful relief as she wrung the seed from his loins. He collapsed on her chest, his panting breath shimmering across her sweaty breasts. He was exhausted, replete.

When his breathing finally slowed, he rolled to lay beside her and pulled up the blanket, his eyes drifting closed.

"Valen?" Her fingers scraped across his scalp as she toyed with his hair.

"Hmm." The heavy pull of sleep was dragging him down, aided by her gentle caresses.

"I love you..."

What? His eyes popped open.

Samara sat on the edge of the bed, looking down at him through her dark lashes, her tousled hair cascading down in waves across her naked body.

She loved him? His heart soared and broke simultaneously. He sat up and looked at her. Did she want him to say it back? That would just prolong the pain for them both when she returned to her homeland. Regardless of how they felt, neither of them could choose love over duty. She knew that.

"Samara..."

She shook her head and put a finger over his lips to silence him. "You needn't say anything. I know it is not what we agreed and naught can come of it, but I wanted you to know."

She loved him. Somehow, it was comforting knowing that the bond they'd forged had touched her too.

He cupped her face in his hand. "We will always have the memories of this time together."

"Já. That we will." She rose and eased her dress over her head, hiding her naked curves from him.

Her revelation made him consider his own feelings. Was he in love with her? It had been so many years since he'd loved Kalda that he couldn't be sure. What he'd had with Kalda had been innocent, pure and naive, but this bond with Samara was ruthlessly honest and entirely different. He fell back into the pillow and sighed. Now he was more confused than ever.

As Samara bent over to pull her boots on, her mussed hair

fell forward to cover her face, but not fast enough to shield her silent tears from him.

His hands fisted in the blanket. He hated that she was hurting. He should have told her he had feelings for her, but he couldn't do it. There was no way that this could last, and it would only hurt her more to pretend otherwise. He would not make it harder for her to leave him behind—he could spare her that pain at least. He sighed and pressed a hand to his chest. Why did he feel hollow inside, as though a bitter tang of regret lingered in his soul?

She crossed the room with a stilted gait, her rigid posture alerting him that something was terribly wrong. She pulled back the drapery and paused. "Goodnight, Valen."

He'd have thought it an ordinary parting whisper were it not for her melancholy tone when she said his name. A dark sense of foreboding settled over him.

"Why does this feel like goodbye?"

Half-hidden by the shadows, she turned to look back over her shoulder at him, her eyes filled with sorrow.

His throat tightened when she shrugged regretfully, starving him of air until his lungs burned. Somehow, he knew before she even spoke, that he had lost her.

"Because it is goodbye," she whispered, and then she was gone.

CHAPTER SEVENTEEN

SAMARA

"*P*rincess!"

Samara looked up from the parchment she was transcribing for the Caliph's records as Ásta stumbled to a stop outside her tent, her auburn hair shimmering like red gold in the late afternoon sun. She carefully placed her quill in the holder on her desk that kept the nibs moist and protected.

"Come quickly," Ásta panted.

"What is wrong?" She rose to her feet, her heart thundering in her chest. Was the island under attack? Was someone hurt?

"They're here. Your handmaidens have arrived."

A strangled gasp escaped her. Adela, Karina, Layal, and Saira. Who had survived?

"Hurry." Ásta motioned her forward impatiently.

She picked up her skirts and ran, following Ásta through the tent encampment, past the guards stationed at the north gate, and all the way to the village center. Would her royal attendants be pleased to see her? Or, would she remind them of all they had lost? To be sure, they would have suffered greatly with Leif and his men. Her stomach churned as she passed though the doorway of the great hall. What would she find within?

Slowly her eyes adjusted to the dim light. Warriors and clanswomen awaiting the evening meal sat at the tables lining the walls, while a cluster of children played a game in the corner with bones and sticks. At the far end of the room, Valen sat on the elevated Jarl's chair, his handsome features grim as he acknowledged her with a somber nod.

She sucked in a shaky breath and followed his gaze to the group of cowering women huddled beside the hearth. Tears welled up behind her eyelids. They lived! All of them.

"Adela." She rushed toward the woman who had cared for her since she was a child and pulled her into an embrace. Thank the stars she was alive! Adela was her rock, her shelter from the storm in the turbulent seas of the royal court. Losing her would have been a crushing blow.

"Princess," Adela whispered, her shoulders shaking as she began to sob.

"Adela..." Her heart ached for her dear friend. She looked into the terrified eyes of the other women huddled behind Adela. "You are safe now. You are all safe."

Karina and Layal flinched, their haunted eyes darting to a commotion near the open door.

Still holding Adela tight, Samara turned to watch her father stride into the great hall, the thundering footsteps of his Haras warriors filling the crowded room.

Every eye in the room followed his commanding presence as he cast his gaze over the handmaidens for visible injuries before continuing toward where Valen sat on the dais overlooking the room.

"Jarl Eriksson."

"Caliph," Valen replied, and nodded respectfully.

"My thanks for the swift return of my daughter's handmaidens. They appear unharmed."

Samara eased Adela from her arms but remained at her side

to offer support. She might not be fierce like Rúna, but she would fight to protect these women from further harm.

Valen nodded at her father. "Já. They are well enough to travel."

Her heart sank—all reason to stay disappeared with the arrival of her handmaidens. Soon, she would have to leave Valen and this island behind and return to her life as the Abassid Princess. There would be no more choosing how to spend her days, no more laughing with Ásta and Rúna, and no more Valen.

"Very good, very good. We shall depart at sunrise."

Her father's words hit Samara like a blade to the chest. Her knees weakened and it felt like she would fall.

"You'll not stay for the festivities?" Valen stepped off the dais, onto equal footing with her father.

Hope sparked within her when the Caliph's eyes flashed with approval at the public display of respect from the Viking leader. It was clear he had come to like the young Jarl in the last few days. Mayhap he would delay a while longer?

"You have been a gracious host, Valen, however our business is concluded. I hasten to return my daughter to the palace so she can be wed."

Nei. Samara pressed her hand over her rolling stomach. She could not bear it. She could not marry for duty. She would wither and die like a flower under the hot desert sun. Before, she may have been able to survive such a fate, but she had changed during her time with the Vikings and there was no going back.

"I cannot, Father."

He turned to face her, his dark brows furrowed in confusion. "You cannot what, Daughter?"

She steeled herself to speak aloud the words that would disconnect her from her people, her lands, her world. "I cannot go home with you nor marry a man I do not love."

"Samara..." he said in warning, shooting her a withering glare.

This time she would not cave to his demands, nor be bullied into submitting to his will. She straightened her back and prepared to fight. Her people had their Caliph, they would survive losing her. She couldn't leave the life she had begun to build with these Vikings, and she couldn't leave Valen. If her father loved her, he would understand.

"I cannot return to the palace. I will not." Her eyes drifted towards the man that had claimed her heart.

Valen stood motionless, looking at her in disbelief.

Her father stiffened, his jaw tensing as he followed her gaze. "What is the meaning of this disobedience?"

"I cannot leave, Papa. I love him."

CHAPTER EIGHTEEN

VALEN

*S*on of Loki! Was Samara trying to get him killed? The air behind him shifted as Rorik moved silently to his side, preparing to defend him. Just last eve she had made it clear that the affair was over and she was leaving.

Her father's face turned a furious shade of red as his head snapped back and forth between the two of them.

Curse the gods! He should have listened to his instincts and stayed away from her. All around the room his warriors rose to their feet, their hands falling to the hilts of their swords, anticipating trouble. If they attacked, there would be mayhem and death. He shook his head and motioned for them to sit. He'd not allow blood to be spilled in his hall.

"YOU WHAT?" the Caliph roared, spittle flying from his mouth.

She'd done it now. He'd been about to attempt to calm the situation, but there was no reasoning with a man in this state. What in Hel was she thinking?

He glanced at where Samara stood, her gaze fixed on her father. Instead of backpedalling or looking contrite, she firmed her lips and jutted her jaw defiantly.

He suppressed a groan. He knew that stubborn look well—there was no way that she would ever back down.

Samara put her hands on her hips and continued. "I love him. I'll not leave."

All of the goodwill he'd built with the Caliph slipped away as the color drained from her father's face. The man was no fool. He would know that his daughter would not make such a claim lightly. He would never believe that naught had happened between them.

"I don't want to marry a stranger. I cannot do it."

He smiled inwardly at Samara's bravery. She was a woman that would fight for what she believed was right, the kind of woman that made a man stronger.

The Caliph pivoted to face him, his glacial glare betraying his barely restrained fury. "Tell her it cannot be or there will be no trade. What say you?"

Valen swallowed hard. His mind was at war with his heart. He could no longer deny that he loved Samara. She'd crept inside his damaged heart and burrowed deep, the warm embrace of her love healing the crushing pain of losing Kalda.

She turned to him, crossed her arms, and stared at him expectantly. He knew she wanted him to declare his affection for her. She would never beg him to claim her, but she knew that in speaking out she was forcing him to choose.

He hesitated. He still had a chance of salvaging these negotiations with the Caliph. If he declared his love now, he would lose his family, his position, and his clan—he couldn't do that. Cursed Freya, for sending him another love that he could not keep. Bile rose in his throat as he choked on the words that would send her away. His eyebrow twitched. His mouth refused to move. He couldn't do it. He couldn't choose.

She blinked and stepped backward. Hurt flashed in her eyes, followed by such apathy that he feared he'd lost her forever.

"A wise decision. The man is not a fool." The Caliph nodded his approval and faced his daughter. "We leave at dawn, Samara."

She crossed her arms over her chest and glared at her father. "I will not go."

"He'll not have you, girl."

The scathing look she shot Valen was like an axe to his aching heart. Gods, he hated hurting her. He clenched his fists to stop himself from buckling and speaking the truth—I want you, I need you, I love you.

She shrugged at her father. "It matters not. In my heart, I know that I belong with the Vikings, to these people. We have forged bonds from the heart, and they have accepted me as one of their own."

Rúna stepped out of the crowd and placed a hand on Samara's shoulder. "There is a place for you with my clan, sister."

"Gratitude, Rúna. I will join you at Luleavst." Samara turned back to her father. "I know you think you know what is best for me, Papa, but I will not marry a man that I do not love."

Óðinn! His chest was cleaving in two. Samara was giving up her home and life to forge a new one in his world. Her bravery knew no bounds. Blessed Freya, he loved this woman so fiercely that it stole his breath away. He loved her... He *loved* her. He could not let her live with Rúna. Sending her home to be wed was one thing, but knowing she lived amongst his kind would kill him.

"Wait!" His shout rolled around the room, quieting the chattering noise of the crowd.

"Son?"

He met his father's concerned stare and held up a hand to stop him from speaking further. His father's words mattered not. He was Viking, not whelp, and mere days away from becoming Jarl. It was long past time he ruled his own life in the same steadfast way he ruled the clan. He had made his decision, and it was final.

"Samara..."

"Já?" She raised an eyebrow at him, clearly still bristling at his refusal to claim her.

He crossed to her and reached for her hand. "I want to make a life with you. Say you will be my wife."

Her eyes softened, but she spoke cautiously. "What of your people? You said that you must marry a Viking bride."

Valen shook his head and glanced at where his father stood. No matter what happened, he would not let her go, ever. "If the clan cannot accept our marriage, then I will step down as Jarl."

A shocked murmur rippled through the crowd, but his father remained silent as though he'd expected this turn of events. He would deal with his father later. He must convince Samara to be his bride now.

He looked into her eyes, letting everything else fall away. It was just the two of them, holding hands, their eyes locked. He let down the walls that protected his heart and let her see all of him.

Her eyes widened as she saw the truth in his heart, but he said it aloud anyway.

"I love you, Samara. I choose you too."

Such was the silence around them that the pitter-patter of the barn cat crossing the room sounded like the thundering heart of Ymir the giant.

The sudden screech of Ivvàr pushing out his chair and rising to his feet broke the quiet. "All who accept this union stand and be counted," he said.

"Nei." He shook his head to halt his brother's foolish act. He could not let Ivvàr, or indeed any who chose to side with him, provoke their father's wrath. He would not tear his clan or his family in two by forcing them to choose.

Ivvàr shook his head firmly. "On this the clan must be heard."

All heads turned to where Rasmus Eriksson stood. Though Valen had increasingly been leading the clan, until the ceremony his father was Jarl and could stop this vote. The tense silence built as the old Jarl considered his son.

Valen held his breath and waited. His father had always insisted that his eldest son marry a bride from another Viking clan. In his mind, that was how it had long been done and his son should follow tradition. Yet Valen had just thrown tradition on the floor and stomped on it in a room full of the most powerful Viking families. No noble Viking bride would have him now. Would his father let the clan decide if they wanted to accept Samara and have him as Jarl?

Slowly, his father nodded at him, though his lips remained pressed together in a hard line. He might not agree, but he would respect his decision and allow this to play out. "The clan will be heard."

"Breathe," Samara whispered, as she squeezed his hand.

He inhaled sharply as his heartbeat raced to a deafening pounding in his ears. His entire future, their entire future, would be decided in the next few moments. Would he lead his clan with the woman he loved by his side? Or would they need to forge a new future for themselves elsewhere?

One by one, chairs scraped across the bare earth as his clan rose to their feet, until every person, including the visiting Jarls and Earls were standing.

His father smiled at him, the worry easing from his face. "Clan Eriksson accepts this union."

His heart soared. Mayhap he could have it all? If Samara would have him. He turned and looked down into her amber eyes. "Do you accept, my love?"

A smile tickled the corners of her mouth. "I heard no question."

He grinned at her teasing. Life would never be boring with her by his side. "You will be the death of me yet, Princess." He clasped both her hands in his. "Samara, my love, will you be my wife and lead clan Eriksson by my side?"

She glanced at where the Caliph stood with his arms folded across his chest, his expression unreadable as his assessing gaze took in everything around him. When she spoke, it was the quiet whisper of a daughter seeking her father's acceptance.

"Father?"

His gaze softened as he looked at his daughter. "All I want is for you to be happy and safe. If this man is willing to give up everything to have you by his side, then I know he will love and honor you, as you deserve. If this is your wish, then so be it."

Valen cupped her chin when her gaze returned to his, and brushed away the steady stream of tears that ran down her cheeks with his thumbs. "What say you, my love?"

She paused, her eyes dancing with delight, and then winked. "Já. I'll be your wife, Viking."

CHAPTER NINETEEN

SAMARA

*S*amara looked around the sacred grove as the first rays of dawn made the frosted green moss shine with an otherworldly beauty. The towering pines overhead sheltered the crowd of witnesses encircling the coronation mound from the cool sea breeze, their evergreen tips swaying in a dance that reminded her of a lover's seduction.

Her rugged Viking warrior stood across from her in his finest garments, his golden hair flowing over the thick black fur cloak that sheltered him from the crisp morning chill. He was beyond handsome, and he was hers.

"Valen."

He smiled down at her, his mesmerizing blue eyes crinkling at the corners.

A blissful glow filled her as she looked at the man she loved, the forbidden Viking that had claimed her heart. She could barely wait to start their life together, a life she was sure would be filled with adventure and long blissful nights in the arms of her Viking Jarl.

She took the cup from the seiðkonur's outstretched hand, her eyes catching on the swirling henna Adela had inked on her hands and feet last eve in the traditional night of henna ritual. She would miss these special moments with her people, but was glad that Adela had decided to stay with her as she started her new life here with Valen.

"Pass him the cup and you shall be wed," said the seer.

Samara glanced down at the flowing green dress Valen's mother had presented to her this morning before she'd settled the bridal crown on her head and welcomed her to clan Eriksson. A deep sense of satisfaction filled her. These were her people now—she belonged here. She traced her thumb over the carved runes etched in the steel cup. This final act would bond her and Valen to a lifetime together.

"I am yours." She raised the cup and drank from it, and then pressed it into his waiting hand. "Drink and be mine."

He drained the cup and passed it to the seer. "I am yours."

"It is time, son, to become Jarl," his father said, and then turned and walked up the coronation mound.

Valen slid his hand into hers, linking their fingers as he led her up the grassy mound to the sacred stone.

Ràsmus Eriksson turned to face the waiting clan. "I cede my place as Jarl of clan Eriksson."

A bird chirped overhead, but the gathered clan remained utterly silent out of respect for the man that had devoted his life to leading them.

"Valen has proven that he will lead with a steady hand and honor. I choose my eldest son as the next Jarl of Gottland." He smiled at Valen and stepped back, the symbolic movement signifying the end of his long reign as Jarl.

Valen nodded at his father, and then turned to face his people and made his pledge. "I vow that Gottland will prosper under my rule. Do you accept me as your Jarl?" The gentle squeeze he gave her hand was the only sign of his nervousness.

She squeezed back, though she knew he worried needlessly.

His people loved him and there was no better man to lead them forward.

A wide grin split his handsome face as the noisy din of swords hitting shields filled the grove. He was Jarl.

"How do you show support for the Jarl pairing?" Ràsmus Eriksson yelled, inciting them further.

Her heart skipped a beat as a roar of voices joined the banging until it reached a crescendo. Her heart filled with such joy that she thought it would burst. They had accepted her too. This was not the home she had been born to, but here with these Vikings, she had found family. This was the home of her heart.

Valen pulled her into his arms and claimed her lips, his tongue teasing and retreating with such vigor that his beard left behind a delicious tingling burn on her skin.

A warm glow of satisfaction filled her as she wrapped her arms around his neck and surrendered to the pleasure. Já. She was exactly where she belonged.

Valen broke the kiss and looked down at her, his heated gaze reflecting the fire she knew blazed in her own. "You are mine now, Princess," he said.

She shook her head and smiled up at him. "Nei. You are mine, Viking."

AFTERWORD

Thank you so much for reading Samara and Valen's story. I hope you had a wonderful time with them. If you enjoyed this book, please consider leaving a review at your place of purchase.

Would you like to hear about my latest news and releases? If so, then sign up for my newsletter at http://www.reethornton.com

If you enjoyed Forbidden Viking, you'll love the other Viking Hearts novellas.

ALSO BY REE THORNTON

BELOVED VIKING

The shield-maiden must marry...

Heir to her father's Jarldom, Rúna Isaksson will soon ascend to replace him as leader, but first she must marry a warrior from another clan to form a powerful alliance. When her father creates a contest to determine the strongest suitor, Rúna demands to compete as well—if she wins, she can choose her own husband. However, she's shocked to discover that her first love is amongst the competitors, the man who abandoned her without looking back. She must not let him win.

A Viking warrior haunted by a dark past...

Jorvan Eriksson has returned from seeking his fortune to claim his childhood sweetheart, but the girl he left behind has become a battle-hardened shield-maiden with no intention of forgiving him. Jorvan has changed too—he now fights a darkness that lurks in his own mind. Somehow, he must conquer his demons to out-manoeuvre the other suitors and win the Viking games for Rúna's hand. Though victory alone will never be enough. He won't settle for anything less than reclaiming the future Jarl's heart.

WINTER VIKING

A Viking queen on the run...

Widow Ásta Helgesen's husband died years ago in a brutal attack that cost her everything she loved. For four years, she has lived as Ásta Oleander, hiding in plain sight as she mourns her husband. The one time she took a man to her furs, the crushing guilt overwhelmed her brief need to move on and she vowed Dànel would be the last. Now the maniacal Jarl who killed her husband has discovered she's alive and is determined to make her his bride. He's dangerous, powerful and will stop at nothing to get what he wants. Forced to flee, Ásta journeys to the bitterly cold northlands to seek sanctuary in the isolated lands of a man she bedded once, and then rejected. Will he protect her from a murderer? Or has she made a terrible mistake?

A warrior with a painful past...

Following the death of his brother, Dànel Kvitfjell has returned to the Sami northlands to take over the shipping fleet that supports the family village. Yet everything reminds him of the tragedy that led to his childhood banishment and he realises that, after more than a decade fostered with Vikings, his family now feel more like strangers. All he wants is to fulfill his duty to his people and return to life with his Viking comrades, but the unexpected arrival of Ásta and her dangerous secrets jeopardizes everything. Why has the woman who rejected his affections sought him out? Forced to flee deep into the wilderness with Ásta, Dànel must confront the painful past that haunts him. Can he protect Ásta from both the man hunting her *and* the harsh winter land where one mistake can steal those you love?

Printed in the USA
CPSIA information can be obtained
at www.ICGtesting.com
CBHW031117120524
8444CB00008B/273